SPUTNIK

Andrew L. Cook was born in Chester in 1996, raised by a family with strong Scouse and Celtic roots. A trained journalist who graduated in 2017 from Liverpool John Moore's University, he went on to live in Catalonia during the independence vote and in Tanzania as a foreign aid volunteer. Alongside these, he has worked in both the north and south of England as he honed his writing style. He currently resides in Gibraltar. Many aspects of his life and experiences can be found in his work. This is his sophomore novel, the first, *The Toucan Man*, was published in July 2021.

You can find Andrew at:

andrewlcookwriter.com

Sputnik

Written by Andrew L. Cook

SPUTNIK

This book is a work of fiction. The Kyshtym Disaster, Mayak, City 40, and the launch of Sputnik 1, however, were very much real - some aspects of which have been altered to fit the narrative but have been treated with the utmost respect and care. The roles played by Nikita Khrushchev and Joseph Stalin in this narrative are entirely fictional, whilst Uncle Sam is in the public domain. Any resemblance to actual persons, living or dead, events, or locales - except the ones mentioned - are entirely coincidental.

For information visit:
https://andrewlcookwriter.com/

ISBN (paperback): 978-1-9196394-2-0

Edited with help from: Charlotte Domokos, Aaron Jackson, Kayleigh Connolly, Mum & Bryn Williams

First edition: November 2022
10 9 8 7 6 5 4 3 2 1

For Scott:

Never let your wild mind grow old.

Wednesday 25th September, 1957.

City 40, Chelyabinsk Oblast, Russian SFSR, Soviet Union.

'Please Mechtatel[1], eat your peas,' Mama asks from the other side of the table; her voice straining, as though she's already tired of talking. I don't listen. Me and Mishka[2] are planning an important mission - far too important to stop and eat peas. Mishka and I don't need to talk in words, we've created a special language that flows through our brains so nobody else can hear what we're talking about. All I need to do is stare into the one button eye he has left and frown my thoughts over to him. His face never changes

---

1 Dreamer.

2 Bear.

when he speaks back, but that's because he's made of fuzz.

'Yuri, stop staring at your bear and listen to your Mama, they would kill to have food like this in Nizhny. We've even got bananas for dessert, but you can't have any unless you eat your peas first,' Papa commands sternly with the crumpled look he always has. Mama says he's got so many wrinkles between his eyebrows because work makes him cross. I've told Papa to work less so many times that I've lost count, but he just tells me that we wouldn't have a house or bananas or Mishka if he didn't work. Worst of all, we wouldn't be building our rocket because he'd be too busy searching for a new job. As long as I don't get gross and wrinkly myself, I don't really mind if he does.

I look towards Vitor; he's rolling his eyes at me. I don't think he wants to be here, I actually don't think Vitor ever wants to be here. Recently, he's been touching noses with a girl outside of his school, pretending they're inuit with big coats on that cover the rest of their faces, enough so only their pale pointy noses poke out. Girls are gross. What if they accidentally touch lips? My tongue spews out of my mouth at the thought. Mama frowns, probably thinking it's directed towards my peas. If she's not careful, she'll get wrinkles like Papa.

'Mechtatel,' a soft hand touches the space between my shoulders gently. Its owner circles shapes across my back with their fingers. It feels nice, so nice that it takes my attention away from Vitor and his rolling eyes.

'How will you ever be a spaceman if you don't eat your peas?' The owner of the hand says, 'You'll need to be big and strong to get there; and they don't pick small boys to go to the Moon, you know.'

Babushka[3]'s right, all the rocket planning can wait until later. I pick up my spoon quickly, catching everyone else at the table off guard. My peas are like asteroids flying through the darkness of space and none shall escape me! I wolf down a big mouthful without a second thought.

Babushka chuckles, she always calls me a 'growing boy', but sometimes I look over at Vitor and think I'd like to stop growing at some point. Maybe I'll ask for less peas next time. Mama's face has stopped furrowing, she's gone back to eating her own dinner. I don't understand why everyone pays so much attention to me eating my dinner and not their own. I watch as Vitor pushes his potatoes around his plate with a fork, slicing them into smaller chunks and squashing them into his plate. The inside of the potatoes are so pale that it looks like they've disappeared into the white of his dish, giving the illusion he's actually eaten them. The real question is, why is his belly so big if he never eats all of his dinner? I bet it's something to do with that girl.

---

3 Grandmother.

My ears twitch at the conversation going on at the other side of the dinner table, but there's nothing interesting worth listening to. Papa's talking about his job again. He works at Mayak, a radio plant on some big hot machine, one that he needs to watch all day apparently to make sure it doesn't get too warm. Why he needs to watch the radio all day when he's at work doesn't make much sense, especially when we've got one here at home that he doesn't bother with. My ears move to the sound of the radio in our front room. Nobody's watching it, never mind listening to it; we only ever do that after dinner. I can hear Korobeiniki[4] playing quietly through the doorway. I like it when my family accidentally leaves the radio on while we're eating, although most of the time I think Babushka does it on purpose just for me. It's much better to listen to music than my family talking, even though they're finally chatting about something interesting.

'So, the Sputnik[5] 1 launch is supposed to happen in just over a week, and according to my colleague, it's making old Uncle Sam sweat.'

Papa had mentioned Sputnik 1 to me on the way home from school today. He said that it'll circle the Earth like the Moon does from somewhere called the LEO, or Lower Earth… something, in space talk. Apparently, the Union is launching it next week. It's

---

[4] Nineteenth-century Russian folk song.

[5] Travelling companion.

being sent to space from a place called Baikonur in the Kazakh SSR. I'm not allowed to tell anyone about it, because it's a secret and even our own government will be angry if they find out that I know. Knowing makes me feel like a spy and gives me a nervous feeling in a good way, I think. That's where my idea of building a rocket came from, that's when me and Mishka discovered that our life goal is to go to space. I don't know who Uncle Sam is or why he's sweating so much, maybe he's the one who'll be riding it into space. I wouldn't be scared; I'd be so excited.

'Papa,' the words fall out of my mouth, 'will the rocket we're building beat Sputnik 1 to space?'

Vitor snorts like a pig, mashed potato escapes the jaws of his mouth like the rabid dog outside that Mama tells me to stay away from. He slaps his hand on the table like he's just heard something funny, causing the cutlery to jangle.

Mama scowls at him and tells him to be quiet, Babushka doesn't even register his laughter. She never places a hand on his back to rub circles, probably because she doesn't like him, definitely not as much as she likes me anyway. Papa's face lights up, he loves it when I talk about science.

'Maybe not as high as Sputnik 1,' he too chuckles like I've said something funny, 'we'll just have to see how far we can get from the living room, hopefully we won't crash into the Urals!'

Babushka swats his leg under the table, wiping the smirk from Papa's face. Whether she wanted me to notice or not, I did. She isn't known for being subtle.

The smile I flash Papa is false. Taking a big mouthful of peas, I hide behind my spoon so he doesn't notice the frown that appears on my face. It isn't good enough, I want to be in space, not close to it, and definitely not lost in the Urals amongst the wreckage of my rocket. Whatever anyone says, I'm going to find a way onto Sputnik 1. I hear Mishka trying to communicate again.

'Not now,' I stare into his beady eye, but he carries on his braintalking anyway.

'I have an idea, I'll tell you before bed,' his bearlike voice grumbles into my thoughts. My brother catches me looking towards Mishka so I nod using my brain. Vitor always laughs when we talk out loud, that's why we created braintalk in the first place.

'One more spoonful of peas please, Mechtatel,' Babushka holds up her own spoon with all her remaining peas on it. My plate still has a lot more on. Sometimes I have to eat all of my vegetables, other times only a few. Either way, I get dessert no matter how many I eat, as long as I have some of them. I scrape my metal spoon across the dirty white of my plate, picking up as many peas as I can. I raise it to my lips and at the same time, me and Babushka shove our spoons into our mouths.

'Mmm,' she hums loudly. To her peas are like cake. I'll never understand how anyone can be so excited for peas, we eat them nearly everyday.

Mama gathers up our plates and takes them into the kitchen, before coming back to the table with a big spotty banana each for us to eat. My stomach rumbles like I haven't eaten any dinner at all, I've always got room for pudding.

***

The rest of dinner is fine. We eat our bananas and go into the living room. We all listen to the music on the radio, me and Babushka dance to *'There Are So Many Golden Lights'* and although she tells me that she doesn't enjoy the lyrics, the tune always makes her want to stand up and dance with me. After that is a speech from Khrushchev. My family disagrees with each other when he's talking. Papa says that he's a man of science and that without him his job at the radio factory and the Sputnik 1 project wouldn't exist, never mind being close to launching into space at all. That makes the Chairman okay in my book, but Babushka says he's a bad man. Apparently, he wants to be friends with sweaty Uncle Sam, and he's said some not so nice things about Red Joe from the posters. But then, Mama says that Red Joe was a terrible man, who used to hurt his own son Yakob and even sold him to the Germans.

After that, Papa normally says how well Khrushchev did in Suez, then Babushka replies saying he looks too similar to a man called Teddy, and as always Mama will try and get them both to be quiet while Vitor sneaks away from the table to go to our room. Most nights normally follow this bedtime story and at this point I can follow it word-for-word. *The Little Gold Key or the Adventures of Buratino* is the best bedtime story though, but by the time I'm actually in bed and ready to be read to, it's so late that nobody wants to sit with me. Instead, they go into their own rooms, probably to fall asleep before Vitor starts snoring.

I think that the world would be a better place if Khrushchev, Red Joe and Sam were friends; then my family might actually read to me before bed, instead of leaving me and Mishka alone with Vitor.

After everyone's disagreements, Mama tells me and Mishka to go and brush our teeth. I gaze in the mirror as I clean them, making sure to scrub every inch of my teeth with my old, fraying brush. I've told Mishka to open his mouth so many times that I've gotten tired of telling him, maybe he's just frightened, or he already has rotten teeth and won't show me. Whenever I ask him questions about it he just ignores me. Two minutes I'm supposed to clean my teeth for, but if you ask me that's far too long. I can race around my mouth in about thirty seconds, getting all of the white parts front and back. Adults have bigger hands that move faster, so why does it take them so long? Two minutes? How slow is that?

'Yuri, bedtime!' Papa shouts. Mishka holds my hand as we walk out of the bathroom to mine and Vitor's room. Vitor hates sharing a room with me, he says that I'm too noisy. If I breathe too loudly, or I cough, Vitor normally hits me with his pillow and pushes me out of my bed onto the cold floor. I tried to do it back to him once, because he snores like a farm animal, but I couldn't roll him off his bed before he realised what I was doing. In the end, he threw me across the room from his bed, back into mine, and threatened to punch me if I tried it again. So, of course I tried again, and of course he punched me. But it was alright, afterwards, Babushka had grabbed him by the ear, dragged him down the stairs of our building and shoved his face into the snow outside.

Vitor has a face where he always looks like he's snarling, like an angry hog in a cage. That must be what happens when you pull stupid faces and the wind blows. Maybe it's just how he always looks at me. I hold Mishka to my chest; my big brother has a habit of stealing him and pretending to throw him out of the window. He got away with it once, throwing Mishka out into the snow and laughing as I cried until morning. That's how Mishka lost his eye. I remember telling Babushka that we should take out one of Vitor's eyes to make it even, she told me that acting like that would make the whole world blind, whatever that means.

He watches me walk past, his face unmoving, like one of those scary paintings in a museum, where even if you hide, they know exactly where you are. This time, he doesn't lunge for me, which isn't surprising. After seeing the girl from school, he normally leaves me alone. I scurry away and dive under my blanket, my friends from school hide from Baba Yaga[6], I hide from Vitor. Our Domovoy[7] never protects me from him, probably because he's my brother, so I wait until his snoring starts, that's when I know it's safe.

When it does, the coast is finally clear for me and Mishka to braintalk.

'What were you trying to say at dinner?' My hands grasp at the blanket we're lying under, trying my best to seal in any sound we might be making from Vitor.

Mishka is quiet for a moment, his face unmoving as he seemingly tries to put his fuzzy thoughts in order.

'We use our rocket as a test, and we send a letter to the government about us going into space on Sputnik 1,' his face doesn't falter as he speaks. Mishka is deadly serious.

---

[6] Slavic Folklore. An ogress who steals, cooks, and eats her victims, usually children.

[7] Slavic Folklore. A house spirit believed to share both the joys and sorrows of a family, who will also warn them of future events.

'Do you really think they'd send an eight-year-old to space?'

Mishka looks at me like he'd laugh if he was able to.

'What else are they going to do? Send a chimp? Or a dog? Plus, adults are too big and heavy to be sent into space.'

He's right, everything he's saying makes so much sense. I hear the roar of Vitor sleeping, the sound startles me, bringing me back from my thoughts and into my bedroom. Vitor's far too large to go to space.

'So, what we need to do is get the address of the government and get in touch with Chairman Khrushchev. He can tell everyone on the radio that we'll be going,' he says, sucking me back into our braintalking. For a bear, Mishka sure is clever.

'Everybody listens to the radio, we'll be famous,' I cover my mouth to hide my pretend scream, 'I'll be the coolest kid at school.'

'Don't forget about me in your letter, Yuri,' Mishka says into my brain.

'I could never,' I smile at him, I like to think he smiles back.

'Well then, that's how we're going to space,' his one eye looks at me blankly, but behind it I can see how pleased he is.

'Perfect, let's start preparing tomorrow,' I snuggle Mishka close; he stops talking when we cuddle. My head pops out of the blanket, causing the room to grow louder, filling my ears with the echoes of Vitor.

I look out of my window into the night sky, the stars above seem to be shining much more brightly than usual. In the middle of it all, the Moon is as white as a fresh batch of pelmeni[8]. I imagine walking across it, the feeling of moon cheese underneath my feet. The idea makes my toes squirm. I wonder what the Earth looks like from the Moon, whether the stars look as pretty from there as they do from here.

Vitor's heavy breath fills the room again, the horrible sound that escapes his nostrils fills every corner of our bedroom. How does nobody else in my family hear him? It surely must keep them awake as well. His chest settles, only to jolt upwards like one of the Urals again, his snoring not graceful enough to give me a steady rhythm.

I think about pushing him off his bed.

---

8 Russian dumplings wrapped in a thin dough.

Thursday 26th September, 1957.

City 40, Chelyabinsk Oblast, Russian SFSR, Soviet Union.

My collar is so unbelievably itchy. I hate my school uniform. Babushka always says that me and Vitor look like *the generals of the future* but being honest I couldn't care less how I look. The collar strangles so tightly around my neck that I feel like my brain is going to pop. I would undo a button the moment I leave our apartment, but the teachers at school always shout when anyone isn't dressed properly. My equally tight, red necktie somehow makes it even worse, because who needs to be able to breathe?

The thick cotton of my long-sleeved shirt sticks to my arms under the weight of my heavy blue coat. I try to itch the top of my arm where it's starting to get moist, yet my fingers can't get past the sewn-on badge. It's too wide and covers most of my arm. The badge is red and shaped like a shield, a white book is opened above what looks like the Sun. My arm screams to be itched, but as uncomfortable and warm as I am right now, I know as soon as me and Vitor leave for school, it's going to be horribly frosty and our sweat beads will freeze over, making my outfit even more uncomfortable.

I watch as Vitor pulls at his collar. When his finger manages to stretch the fabric away from his skin, it reveals a thick red mark where it's been strangling him. The second I see it, the collar snaps back to his neck like an elastic band, leaving him gasping for air again. Watching him makes me feel more uncomfortable, I squirm at the thought of my own throat. Why school uniforms are made this way, I'll never know.

Papa's uniform looks much more comfortable than ours. He's already left for work with his loose fitting white coat and funny white hat. When he comes home, I like taking the hat off his head and running away with it. I never actually want the hat for myself, I just enjoy him chasing me around the house to get it back. I normally hide in my parents' wardrobe or under their bed, mainly because it's the one time I can get away with going in there. After a while, the floor will creak loudly under Papa's footsteps. He'll make his voice low and gruff, just like

Mishka's. He always says that Poschekotat' Ruku[9] is coming for me. That's when the real fun starts, when he crouches onto all fours and runs towards my hiding place like a wild animal. Somehow, he always knows where I am, even though I try my best to be really quiet.

Poschekotat' Ruku is the name Papa gives to his hand when it's being taken over by the monster that lives inside it. All it wants to do is find me and tickle me until I let go of his hat. When the monster takes over, Papa walks around the house holding Poschekotat' Ruku with his other hand, trying to hold it back. He even rolls around on the floor shouting for my help while I'm hiding. I never fall for it, because I know it's just Poschekotat' Ruku pretending. Papa's never successful in holding it back and I always end up on the floor, laughing as it tickles the soul out of my body, having found me like it always does.

The sizzling of butter from the frying pan brings me back to our breakfast table, the smell reminding me that we're just about to eat. Breakfast is my favourite meal of the day, especially during the autumn. Mama makes her own jam from the blackberry bush outside, and it might be the best thing I've ever tasted. I'm not allowed to eat the blackberries straight from the bush outside because then us and all of our neighbours have less jam for

---

9 The Tickle Hand.

the winter. I still try to take them when Mama isn't looking, but she's got eyes like a hawk, or ones in the back of her head. I can't decide which one is more likely. Sometimes though, when I really want one, Babushka sneaks one into her pocket when she's helping Mama gather them to give to me later. It's like she knows when Mama's hawk eyes aren't on alert and when to strike. Babushka's the best, but she already knows that.

Mama plates up the jam with some freshly fried eggs, I can already taste the sweet paste mixing with the popped runny egg in the bowl. It makes my tummy squeal with delight. I glance over at the drool starting to form around Vitor's greasy lips. Mama's jam and eggs is one of the few things we actually agree on.

Babushka doesn't like eggs, fresh ones anyway. She says that they give growing boys bad immune systems and fragile muscles and that they're much healthier when they're powdered. I'm not sure how anyone could powder an egg, they're so gooey? You'd just get yolk everywhere. Papa tells me not to listen to her, but then who would steal blackberries for me if I ignore her? I just pretend to agree, then eat my runny eggs when Mama plates them up with jam. That way everyone wins.

It's no question that I need to be big and strong to go to space, and Papa *is* the scientist after all, so I think I'm going to go with what he says. He eats the same as me and Vitor, and his brain is so powerful that it got him a job as a scientist. Mama says that's a very big deal, so I also think it's a very big deal. So much of a big deal in fact that he had to move out here by himself for years before we were allowed to follow him. Very important radios indeed.

I watch as Mama brings over my plate of eggs and jam, I can feel my tongue licking my lips like it's got a brain of its own. She places it down in front of me. I start attacking it straight away with my fork, giving my breakfast no mercy, no chance of survival.

'Mechtatel, slow down, you're going to give yourself indigestion,' she ruffles my blond hair, causing my head to wobble.

Everyone at home calls me Mechtatel, everyone except Vitor at least, who calls me Yuri when everyone else is around, but when they're not he calls me mean things Mama says I'm not allowed to repeat; unless I want my mouth washed out with soap anyway. Babushka gave me the name Mechtatel back when I wasn't old enough to remember anything. She says it means *dreamer* and that when I was a baby I always looked like I was thinking about something else, and that I was never paying attention. Babushka's convinced that I've been here before, on Earth I mean, as a different person in a different time. That doesn't make any sense to me, surely I'd remember something from then, unless my baby memories got mixed up with my old life memories and as I grew up I forgot them all. What are the chances of that though? I was probably just looking around for some food, or Mishka before he lost one of his eyes. Or maybe Vitor, because when I was little he would…

'Mechtatel!' Mama brings me back to the table again. Apparently, I've been eating too slowly now. She just told me to slow down.

'Vitor is leaving in a minute, finish your breakfast and put your shoes on,' she tuts as she starts to clear away everyone else's plates.

I wolf the food into my mouth, oozing yolk dribbles from my lips down to my chin as I chew as fast as possible. My teeth squelch as they move, the fruity egg in my mouth is delicious. I hear the door unlock, causing my head to jolt in the other direction. I look straight at Mama, who's holding my chin with her hand.

She attacks my face with a napkin, the rough paper hurts my chin as she wipes away all of the egg juice. I try my best to retreat, but I can't get away, nothing can break her iron grip. The cleaning stops and my lids open, her big blue eyes stare right into mine.

'Vitor is leaving, put your shoes on,' she says as she kisses my forehead.

I run over to the door, still chewing as I slide on my old leather shoes. Why doesn't Mama worry about indigestion when I'm in a rush? Vitor hasn't even bothered to close the door, the cold air that lingers in the space between apartments makes itself at home in our doorway. I grab my bag and go to leave.

'I love you both!' Mama shouts. Shouting it back, I slam the door accidentally before running down the stairs of our building to catch up with Vitor, who seems to be trying his very best to get as far away from me as possible.

***

Trying my hardest not to slip over on the icy ground, I make my way towards Vitor. He's already tearing the red necktie from his throat, having undone the top button before I'd reached him. The colour returns to his cheeks almost instantly, letting his face relax as much as his angry eyebrows allow him to. I try to slot my fingers behind my own collar, it won't even budge the slightest bit. Watching Vitor free himself from his shirt makes my neck hurt even more. I could easily take off my tie, that's not the problem, it's trying to put it back on comfortably before getting to school. I don't want Mama to get shouted at on parents' evening in a couple of weeks, I've seen it happen to Vitor and he pays for it massively when he gets home. All I can do is try and forget that I'm being strangled to death.

I start running towards a big iced-over puddle on the pavement in front of me, sliding across it and reaching Vitor. He's already retying his necktie. The sweat on my body that had built up at home is already starting to go cold.

'Um Vitor, can you help me loosen mine?' I pull my necktie towards him hesitantly, doing so tightens it even more, which I didn't think was possible. After finishing his own, he looks down at me like I've just dropped a brick on his bare toes.

'No, and walk behind me mu-dak[10], I don't want anyone seeing us together,' he snaps. I sigh and tuck my tie back into my coat, defeated. I watch as Vitor slips slightly on the icy walkway, I laugh quietly so he can't hear me. Although not-so-deep down I wish he would've fell flat onto his fat, ugly, stupid face.

We approach the corner of our street where two girls are waiting. One of them is the girl that Vitor likes to touch noses with. I've never seen her waiting for him here before. She's plump-looking, a similar shape and size to Vitor really, her hair dark and tied into pigtails with ribbons that bloom like white lilies. The decorations in her hair are part of the girls' school uniform; as is the rest of her attire, a black dress with white lace over it and a thick woolly coat to top it all off. It's so annoying that all the boys have to dress like military men, and they get to dress like they're staying at home all day. If I could choose, I think I'd wear the dress, but I'd never tell anyone that. Especially not Vitor.

---

10 Idiot.

Behind Vitor's 'friend' is a smaller girl, around the same height as me. I recognise her from my class; it's Nastya. She looks like the older girl but less plump, naturally showing off more of her facial features. She wears the same uniform as what I assume is her older sister. Nastya always looks at me weirdly at school, and I always catch her when she's trying to dart her eyes away from me, normally when I'm doing school work or drawing. It's creepy, if she wants to talk to me, why doesn't she just do it? I'm not scary, I'm just Yuri, or Mechtatel, or whatever.

The older one squeals and shuffles towards Vitor in baby steps, trying her best not to fall over on the slippery ground. Nastya waves at me, well, I think she does. She isn't looking at me properly, her eyes seem to be looking everywhere else but towards me. I look behind me, gazing down the road that me and Vitor had just walked up, yet there's nobody there. When I turn back she giggles like I just did something funny, just wait until Mishka hears about this.

'Hi Polina, I missed you last night, as always,' Vitor says as he opens his arms to welcome her. His voice sounds so different when he speaks to her, the venom that normally swirls around his words isn't there, like it's being saved for us all at home. It's then that I notice that he's never mentioned her name at home, not to me, not to Mama or Papa, not even to Babushka. She gives him a bearlike cuddle, then her eyes fall to me. I half-expect the worst, a Vitor twin who's going to call me a mu-dak, pull on my tie and push me over on the black ice. To my surprise she squeals again, causing my ears to ring like I'm standing under the school bell when it goes off between lessons.

'Vitor! I didn't know little Yuri was your brother!' She scurries over and ruffles my hair, causing it all to fall out of place, not even giving me a moment to think about how she knows my name. I manage to catch a glance of her through the hair that now lives across my face, her eyebrows furrow like Papa's. My hand is still pulling at the collar of my uniform without me realising.

'Oh, little one, is your collar too tight?' she smiles an honest smile. All I can do is nod, and even that's done poorly thanks to the fact I can't move my neck properly. In a flash she loosens my necktie, undoes my top button and pushes it closer to my neck, giving the illusion of being done up correctly.

'Better?' she giggles in the same pitch as her little sister, I nod with a lot more freedom than I had before. It feels like my head is slowly re-joining my body, having been separated from it while getting dressed this morning. Vitor's snarling behind Polina, with a look that says '*just you wait until we get home, that bear of yours is going to get it*'. She actually seems quite nice, why does she want to touch noses with someone as rotten as him?

'Nastya speaks about you all the time! You can walk to school together, we'll be just behind you!' she smiles as Nastya strolls over awkwardly, almost on queue. Polina goes to talk to Vitor pretty much the moment she arrives. I can overhear her ask him why his collar was unbuttoned and mine wasn't. Polina pulls Papa's face again. Vitor's cheeks go bright red, as though the top button was still choking him. I really hope he doesn't push me out of bed later, because I know that somehow this will be my fault, it always is.

'Hi, Yuri,' Nastya chirps in my direction. Why does this family all seem to sing their words like birds who have just discovered their voice? Her grey eyes are instantly much prettier up close compared to when they stare at me from across the classroom. Wait a minute, my thoughts finally catch up with me.

'Why do you talk to your sister about me?' Now it's my turn to pull Papa's face.

'I was just talking about everyone in class last night at dinner. It wasn't just you, I promise! It was Gertruda, and Dimitri and Marlen too," her face goes as red as my tie. I can hear Polina giggling to herself and whispering to Vitor as we're walking down the road.

'O-okay,' I say, suddenly feeling awkward for some reason. The sound of Dimitri's name makes me feel sick to my stomach, he's the last person I'd ever want to talk about at dinner. Other than Vitor of course, but I can't escape him at home.

'What did you do last night?' She asks me suddenly.

'If you must know, I'm going to be building a rocket, so last night I was forming my plan on how to do it,' I place my hands on my hips confidently, pulling my head back so I can look at her down the barrel of my nose. Her eyes might as well have stars in them.

'You're building a rocket? Wow,' she's acting weird again.

'Yes Nastya, I just told you that,' I can overhear my older brother and Polina snickering.

'That's so cool, where are you going to go?' Her fingers grow all fidgety as she talks, like she's playing cat's cradle without any string.

'To space,' I offer bluntly.

Nastya squeaks with excitement, catching me off-guard as she lets out a little jump. When she lands, her feet fall onto a thick piece of frost, causing her to wobble. Nastya slips on the ice, instinctively grabbing my arm for support. I try my best to stay upright while simultaneously attempting to stop her from falling, but she's already gone, pulling me down with her. We crash onto the floor of the icy road, spinning like tops on the frosted dew that coats the ground. Polina scurries over, dropping to the ice on her knees to check if we're alright. Vitor's laughing loudly, because of course he is.

***

We separate from Vitor and Polina once we get to school. After Nastya had pulled me down to the frozen pathway, Polina had rushed over to help us get back up again. Vitor hadn't, seemingly enjoying the sight me sliding around on the ice like a new-born deer. Luckily neither of us got hurt, although Nastya is now not talking to me properly, after what only felt like moments of her acting normal for once. Vitor, after taking a brief pause from laughing, had said that she's probably just embarrassed, which is obvious, because she just pulled me down on the ice. Thanks for nothing, mu-dak. They'd dropped us off at our elementary school and watched us walk inside before holding hands and walking towards their big secondary school, thinking that nobody was watching them. I was, and I can't help but think that Polina sees a different Vitor to everyone else, maybe she bought a pair of those rose-tinted glasses Babuskha says Mama bought Papa.

Walking through the gates with Nastya, before I can even try and start a conversation, she runs off towards her friends Katarina and Gertruda without saying anything that sounds remotely like 'goodbye'. I'm not sure what I've done to make her run off like that, if anything she's the one who owes me an apology for pulling me over and now, she's the one being rude. I don't know, everyone in that family seems to make baffling decisions. I watch as she makes her way towards them both, slowing down as she gets further away from me. They both wave at her, before they give me a slight, if not confused smile as to why she's leaving my company so abruptly. Katarina and Gertruda both have the same dark-coloured hair Nastya has, all three styling it the same way with their white lily bows. When they all have their backs to you, you honestly can't tell which one is which from a distance, but when they're together, I can always tell Nastya apart. The other two just don't stand out to me at all. My best friend Marlen can always tell which one Katarina is, but can't tell the difference between Nastya and Gertruda. It's strange when I think about it really.

My walk ends suddenly with a thud, like I've accidentally walked face first into a brick wall.

The *wall* has venomous eyes, and they're staring at me. Dimitri. I know the look I'm getting all too well, it's when people don't like me too much. I've had enough practice receiving it from Vitor. Honestly, I've given up trying to change anyone's mind, what's the point? They either start liking the fake version of you that you're putting on, or you look like a complete fool for trying.

In the cold morning, steam blows out of Dimitri's nostrils like an angry bull. He's even got a name that sounds mean, Dimitri. His head looks like an egg, on account of being the only bald kid in school. I'd ask him why, but he'd probably punch me in the face. He forces his palm into my chest, causing me to stagger back onto my other leg.

'Morning mu-dak,' he says, speaking to me exactly like Vitor does. I look up at him, his face has one of those stupid smiles you wish you could wipe off with a wet sponge. My eyes glance down, in his school uniform he already looks like a KGB[11] officer, all he's missing is the red beret. In a couple of years, I think the teachers will listen to him rather than the other way around. Behind him is the part-human, part-rat, Mikhail. He likes to refer to himself as a bully, but all he actually does is watch Dimitri push other kids around before saying he did it himself. In a way, it's like Mikhail takes credit for Dimitri's homework, which makes sense considering I'm fairly sure Mikhail actually does Dimitri's homework. It makes you wonder whether one could survive without the other, probably not. There's a word for weird relationships like that, we learned it in biology, but I can't remember it.

'Morning, I'm actually trying to get to class,' I try to end our conversation and walk away before it starts, leaving this situation without me in it.

[11] Security agency of the Soviet Union.

However, Dimitri puts his unfairly large man-like arm in the way, blocking me with ease. His family must be weightlifters of some sort, that or his Mama's a brown bear.

'No you don't,' Mikhail says for some reason, almost like he's forgotten it's Dimitri's arm and not his that's in my way.

'Did I see you walk into school with Nastya today?' Dimitri asks, his arm hanging in the air, if it was me, I'd have definitely gotten tired and had to put it back down by now.

'Yeah, my brother and her sister are friends.'

'Friends?' Dimitri raises half the hair on his head, that being one eyebrow.

'Yeah, can I go now?' I try to duck under his arm, he lowers it slightly to stop me again. I don't even try to force my way past it.

'No, not yet,' Mikhail snickers again.

'Looks like more than friends to me,' Dimitri laughs, 'that's fine, Nastya would have picked me anyway, but she won't even look at you now because siblings can't go out with siblings. That's just gross.'

Looks like I wasn't the only one who saw Vitor and Polina holding hands.

'Yeah,' Mikhail imitates the bigger boy's laugh.

'Great, I'm not interested anyway,' I finally shove past him and start walking away, in return I receive a hard push in the back, causing me to jolt forwards; his touch nowhere near gentle.

'Stay away from her. I'll be watching you at Gertruda's party on Saturday,' Dimitri snaps, turning to look at the trio of girls. They're all giggling amongst themselves. Nastya seems to have gone back to normal after our incident. Her eyes look to Dimitri, then to me. Our eyes meet but hers dart away faster than our fall to the ground this morning. Back to normal indeed.

I hear Dimitri huff, which his sidekick imitates as I walk away from them. I swear this school is full of chudaks[12].

***

I watch as the new boy at school wrestles with the collar of his uniform. He looks so uncomfortable; he doesn't have a Polina to undo his top button for him. I'd seen him around at lunch, but hadn't spoken to him, if anything he seems so away with the fairies that he doesn't want or need any human interaction. Now me, Marlen, Gertruda, and him are sitting at a table together in Russian class, we always get moved around in different lessons to work with everyone.

The new kid looks kind of Chinese, but not really, he also doesn't look very Russian, but has Russian characteristics. He looks like a mixture of the two, and his accent doesn't sound like anything I've ever heard before either. He's speaking in a language I

12 Weirdos.

don't understand under his breath, I can't turn my ears away, it's like listening to a foreign radio.

'What language are you talking in?' Gertruda asks, my face jolts with a look of panic for a moment, like it was me who'd said it out loud. Part of me always worries that other people can braintalk too, which would be so embarrassing, especially in front of a girl.

'Sorry,' he says in our language, 'It's Kazakh, my dad and I just moved here from Tyuratam,' he drops his hands to the table and starts tapping his fingers, leaving little wet dots where his hands are sweating. His eyes don't move from Gertruda.

Me and Marlen watch what's happening with intrigue. Marlen's blond like me, so we look pretty similar, but when he stares at things for too long his lazy eye kicks in and it runs off to look at something else, meaning he has to look around the room to keep it from doing so. That's what he tells me at least, Babushka says she thinks something's wrong with him.

Kazakh. I think to myself, I've definitely heard that before. I can't recall where though.

Gertruda smiles at Alikhan and goes back to writing in her notebook. I don't think she enjoys being enrolled at the boys' school. Girls were only allowed to join a few years ago, before then we didn't have any in our year. The three of them had all joined at once and have been best friends since. I'm still getting used to having them around. I mean, I really enjoy having them around, I say to myself in case she can braintalk too. Her eyes don't move from her book, and her face remains in the same expression. Either she definitely doesn't braintalk, or she's a really good liar. Who knows which one is the truth.

'My name is Alikhan,' the new boy throws his hand forward to shake hers. She takes it carefully, shaking it lightly while trying to hold as little of it as possible, definitely because of his sweaty hands. I catch Marlen's lazy eye looking around the room.

'Gertruda,' she lets go as his hand crawls back towards its owner like a spider. He smiles widely.

'My name is Marlen,' my friend sprawls across the table like Alikhan had just done, but with his teeth sticking out to make him look goofier. He imitates his accent to the point where it feels uncomfortable. I feel bad, but I laugh along anyway because he's my friend. Getruda laughs because she thinks it's funny.

The genuine smile disappears from the Kazakh's face. Elsewhere, other tables of kids who were listening-in laugh along as well, quiet enough so that Mrs. Palakova doesn't hear them, but loud enough to let Alikhan know that he's made a fool out of himself. My stomach feels weird, like Vitor has sucker-punched me in the gut, or I've eaten some of Papa's cooking. Alikhan's eyes fall on me.

I try to give him an encouraging smile.

'Yuri,' I shoot him a thumbs up, which he returns. Mrs. Palakova shushes the rest of the room, finally noticing all the commotion and tells us to concentrate on our books. Alikhan doesn't say anything else to us for the rest of the day, most likely out of fear of being picked-on again.

***

'So, she grabbed your arm and pulled you to the ground with her?' Mishka says shocked, like he can't believe what he's hearing.

'I know, all I was doing was walking next to her. I told her about the rocket and she fell, pulling me down with her!' I look into his last buttoned eye, I swear I catch his face frowning, everyone seems to be giving me that look today.

'You told her?' His braintalking is serious, like his permanently grumpy sewn-on face.

'Yeah? Why?'

'She'll get jealous. Girls can't go to space.'

I fold my arms. I've never thought about that. Mama and Babushka haven't been interested in building the rocket at all. All of the parts are waiting in the front room, yet they told me I have to wait for Papa to come home from work before I can start. It's the only reason I'm talking to Mishka right now. Vitor's out with Polina, so this is the perfect time to start building the rocket without him coming back and trampling all over it.

'Maybe you're right, but what's wrong with her knowing about it?' I ask my bear; he replies much quicker than I thought he would.

'She might tell Dimitri, or she might be a spy, from Britain, or West Germany, or America,' his words shock me like a cold winter morning.

Before I can respond, the lock on the front door begins to turn. I run down the hallway as fast as I can. I launch onto Papa and hug him with the squeeze of a thousand Mishka's. He laughs and walks me into the living room as I hang from his belly. His uniform is rough and dirty and it scratches my face like an unkempt beard. Papa's eyes are gentle but tired. He ruffles my blond hair, taking the hat from his own head and popping it on top of my own.

'Run,' he mouthes, before looking at his hand in terror.

'Poschekotat' Ruku,' I gasp, letting go of his tummy and rushing into Mama and Papa's room, holding the hat tightly with all of my might. I dive under their bed and wait for the hand to come and get me. I tremble with excitement; I can hear him say hello to Mama and Babushka before he runs in the room shouting loudly about the monster taking over his hand.

'Eeeeeeeek,' I scream as he drags me out by my feet and tickles my chest with his strong fingers, before pulling up my shirt, revealing the white of my belly and raspberrying my stomach. I throw the hat back at him but he doesn't stop, making me laugh so much I start to cry. He picks me up after the torture's over, throwing me over his shoulder by my legs and carrying me towards the kitchen like a sack of potatoes, chanting about how Poschekotat' Ruku is going to eat me for dinner. My head rocks back and forth as I watch the world sway upside down, wondering how anything could be as fun as this.

'Let's get to work on our spaceship, Mechtatel,' Papa says, somehow making everything even more fun.

I'm so excited I could burst. Papa throws me face-first onto our old tatty couch, giving me a mouthful of fabric as I collide into it. Turning around, I spit out the fluff that had travelled away with me. That's when I see it, the slab of cardboard that dreams are made of. I hear Babushka say from the kitchen that she'd found it outside of a shop in the centre and had taken it for me. Next to it is the last of the crinkled metal roofing that was leaning against the wall outside our building, alongside three big pots of paint. A red like my school badge, yellow like the tools painted on the Soviet flag and blue like the sky when the sun is shining. It's going to look brilliant, so much so that the spacemen on Sputnik 1 will want to fly with me on my rocket, not the other way around.

I look up towards Papa, who seems ecstatic at my reaction. He rubs his hands together, seemingly eager to start working on our project. He pulls himself to a kneel, grabbing a sheet of cardboard and attempting to start on the rocket. It's only then that we notice Mama in the doorway, tutting.

'There's no way you're painting in here Alexei, go to the other room,' Papa looks up at her with his usual face, sighing before grabbing the cardboard and the roofing and carrying it into the kitchen. I can hear him huffing loudly, like he's trying to make it sound a lot more difficult than it actually is.

I try to lift one of the tins of paint to carry it through for Papa while he's in the other room. I can only manage to get it off the floor a little bit, even as I try as hard as I can with both hands. It's so heavy that I drop it with a loud thud. I can hear the paint sloshing around inside, luckily it hasn't been opened yet so it doesn't spray all over our living room. I decide to leave it alone, it's probably better if Papa does it himself. I don't want to get into trouble with Mama.

Papa comes back in and grabs all three easily, putting me to shame. When he leaves again, I tense my arm into a curl and poke at my muscle, my finger is close to bursting right through to the other side. I can't believe how strong he is sometimes. This is exactly why I eat my eggs in the morning, but they don't seem to be working yet. Maybe I should eat the weird, powdered ones like Babushka says, maybe the gooey eggs are making my arms gooey too. I follow him through to the other room, sitting with him on the floor to start.

'Oh Mechtatel, before I forget,' Papa smiles at me, 'I've got a new colleague at work and he has a son around your age, we're going to invite them both over for dinner tomorrow. Hopefully you and his son can be friends.'

'Okay,' I say, his words going in one of my ears and out the other. I can't tear my attention away from the cardboard in his hands. We've not even started, and I already want it finished.

'Great. Let's get started, shall we?' He says before asking me how it should look, then realising he's left the glue behind, running off to the living room once more.

This is going to take forever.

Friday 27th September, 1957.

City 40, Chelyabinsk Oblast, Russian SFSR, Soviet Union.

'You should see it Marlen, it's so cool. Papa glued together all of the pieces so you can sit inside it, and you can fold the lid over so no air can escape when you're in space,' I can't and won't stop my face from looking so excited. He's not really listening though; his concentration is focused on throwing pebbles against the school wall. When he opens his mouth, he doesn't even ask about my rocket.

'Do you think Katarina thinks about me as much as I think about her?'

I throw my pebble harder than his into the wall in response.

'I don't know Marlen. I swear all everyone ever talks about nowadays is girls.'

He shoots me a disgusted look, like I'm the one who's offending him! He's the one who's ignoring me! Why does nobody talk about cool things like space, or tanks, or action figures anymore? Last year was fine, we all used to play together and pretend we were soldiers in the playground, or demons and angels fighting over Earth, or knights chopping the heads off of dragons.

Even the girls were fun to play with once, joining in with all our games. Now they just stare and giggle and act weird when they think no one's looking. When the boys are around them, they act weird too, sometimes I wish that we were all separate again, not that they're mean or anything, I don't know. It just feels like they're from space, maybe they were replaced over the summer break by aliens, which could be why they all act so creepy now. But then again, all my friends do as well. What if I'm the only one left? Maybe I'll find the aliens when I go to space with Mishka and then I can ask them.

My panic is interrupted by Marlen, who throws a pebble at the wall again with a smirk on his face. Looks like he'd noticed how hard I threw mine and made sure that his stone chipped off part of the brickwork.

There aren't a lot of toys at school, so at breaktime we normally throw pebbles at the wall and talk until we go back inside to stare mindlessly at books again. There are some cool metal tanks and jeeps but some of the older kids are playing with them right now, as they normally do. If I've learnt anything from Vitor, it's that older kids don't share. He's probably the Dimitri of his class, I wonder if he's got a Yuri, or do I get the *pleasure* of being the only one?

I hear a shoe scuff on the floor and turn around to see Alikhan standing awkwardly on his own. Marlen, bored of his pebble throwing, follows my eyes to gawk at where I'm looking.

'He's so weird. All he talks about is science and speaks to himself in his strange little language,' Marlen holds up a pebble to hurl at him but decides at the last minute to throw it at the wall instead. Not because he didn't want to, but because he isn't in the mood for a ruler to lash across his knuckles.

I'm struggling to understand why he's so angry at Alikhan. He seems fine, just out of place and a little different. And anyway, what's wrong with science? I want to talk about space and science, Marlen's the weird one being obsessed with Katarina and the rest of them. I glance back at Alikhan, his fingers fiddling like something is between them, his hands darting in and out of his pockets awkwardly enough to tell anyone paying attention that something is wrong.

He notices us staring and runs off behind a wall where we can't see him, poor kid, his fidgeting is probably going crazy behind there.

'Freak,' Marlen says, before his eyes wander to the girls across the playground.

'Should we go and talk to them?' He winks.

'No,' for the first time in my life I wish the bell would ring.

'Why not, do you love boys or something? They'll have you arrested for that. Thrown in the gulag[13], and they'll chop off all your fingers. I bet you want to wear dresses as well.'

I pretend to know what a gulag is, before looking down at my hands and wiggling my fingers around. I don't want to lose them; how would I be able to write my letter? It's not like I'm attracted to boys or anything, I just don't care about girls - what's so wrong about that? My mind wanders back to my fleeting thought about wearing a dress instead of my uniform yesterday morning, it isn't like I actually wanted to - it just seems much more comfortable. Wait, is Marlen another braintalker who can hear thoughts? I study his face; he's just waiting for me to respond. This is the second time in as many days this has happened, from now on I'll have to be extra careful about what I'm thinking, who knows who's listening.

Marlen, seemingly agitated with our conversation, has already jumped to his feet with his hand out towards me, knowing that I'll cave and agree to whatever he says. Especially with what he's just

---

13 Forced labour camp.

said I can't really turn around and say no. He knows what he's doing, he's naughty like that. Mrs. Palakova tells me all the time to stay away from him, but it's difficult when you've been friends with someone for so long. How are you supposed to explain to your oldest friend – who isn't Mishka - that you don't want to talk to them anymore without them getting upset, or angry? I'm not sure which one of those is worse, they both sound awful.

Suddenly, the urge to steal the tanks from the older kids becomes much more appetising. I'd rather them chase me around, threatening to beat me up than go over there, anything but that. I look over towards them, laughing, playing, making noises as if the tanks are real. I'm so jealous. I begrudgingly take Marlen's ungrateful hand and silently follow him over to the girls. My feet drag across the floor. I feel like I'm being made to do chores at home.

Nastya notices us walking over first, because of course she does, nothing ever escapes her forever watching eyes. Her vision darts around like she's trying to catch a fly by looking at it. The other two haven't stopped their conversation for long enough to notice us walking over. I hate this, it's so awkward. I search around for anyone else to talk to; it's only Dimitri and his little companion Mikhail watching us walk over to them. Ugh. I swear they don't even talk to each other, it's like they spend all of their time guarding everyone else from talking to the girls. Why did Alikhan have to go and hide behind that wall?

'Hi girls,' Marlen says, leaning on Gertruda's shoulder with his elbow, trying way too hard to be cool.

She pushes his arm off her quickly, understandably annoyed at his sudden interruption.

'Hi Marlen,' Katarina says, ignoring me completely, as she always does when he's around.

Gertruda huffs loudly, obviously unhappy at being ejected from the conversation she was once in. I feel her pain, I really do. The awkwardness of this situation feels like a knife in my heart. I look down at my leather shoes, not noticing until now how scruffy they are. I make a mental note to ask Mama to shine them with me soon, which is fine because it's one of my favourite things to do with her. When I'm not looking, she taps me on the shoulder and dabs the black paste on my nose when I turn around to look at her. I always try to get her back, but my arms are too short to reach.

I put my hands in my pockets and try to zone out of this awful conversation. My mind wanders to my rocket waiting patiently in my living room. In the end, Mama had made us move it back because we were in the way when she was trying to cook dinner. She only let us carry on under the condition that we covered the front room carpet with newspaper though, which we did – even though it used up valuable painting time.

Papa's friend's son better like to paint because that's what we're doing tonight. It needs to be finished, no ifs or buts. My rocket needs to be ready for launch tomorrow because I can't launch on a school day, because I'm in school, obviously. That reminds me, I need to write my letter to Khrushchev too. That can wait though, Mishka and I need a successful launch before asking to join the space program. I just need to find an address to send it to. I pull Papa's frown face, I have no idea who to ask to get it, maybe Mrs. Palakova knows?

'Sorry about pulling you over yesterday,' a quiet voice tells me, I know it as Nastya's straight away - something about the sound of her voice. My frown disappears almost instantly.

I turn to look at her, she looks like a whimpering puppy. Maybe because she looks so frightened about what answer is going to leave my lips, maybe because I genuinely don't mind, but I've forgiven her for yesterday. I don't have any scrapes or bruises and to be honest I haven't even thought about the incident since telling Mishka last night.

'It's fine, no harm done.'

A smile returns to her face. Gertruda huffs again, louder this time, in an effort to drag all of the attention onto herself no doubt. I'm not sure what she's moaning about now, but she's always been that kid in a room who's got something to moan about, normally when she's not in the spotlight. She walks off to another area of the playground, seemingly towards Dimitri and Mikhail.

'Are you still working on your rocket?' Nastya asks.

Oops. I forgot that she knew. I must be more careful.

'Yeah, Papa and I put the base together last night. Tonight, we'll be painting it,' I fold my arms proudly.

'Wow, and when will you launch it?' Her eyes shine like the shooting stars I hope I'll see when I get to space.

'Well, tomorrow morning is Gertruda's birthday party, so I'm thinking it'll be in the afternoon. I'm too excited to wait until Sunday,' the calculations whir through my head. Actually, I really do need to get that address today.

'I'm not doing anything on Saturday afternoon,' Nastya hints without an inch of subtlety. She's beaming a smile brightly towards me, waiting for an invitation.

It's just like Mishka had warned me. Girls can't go to space; he told me so. I need to think of a response that says no but doesn't hurt her feelings.

'O-oh. I don't think that's going to work.'

Her smile shatters like a broken mirror.

'What? Why?' Her face droops.

'Girls can't go to space,' I can feel Mishka's grizzly voice coming out in my own, making me feel like an alien in my own body. The moment his words come out; I know I've said something I'll immediately regret. It's too late though, like squeezing a tube of toothpaste - it's impossible to put my words back where they'd come from.

It's fine though, right? She won't be mad - Mama and Babushka stay at home, they aren't interested in my rocket, or Sputnik 1, so she won't be that bothered either. It's not wrong, that's just how it is. Papa never mentions any girls working at the radio factory. I'm just helping her out. Yeah, if anything I'm stopping her from getting her hopes up too high.

Marlen and Katarina have stopped talking and are just listening to us. I hate this, I wish we were still throwing rocks at the school wall.

Her face changes almost immediately, from puppy to grizzly bear in the blink of an eye. She's angry, furious even. It's the face Mama pulls when Papa comes home too late and stumbles through the door, slurring his words. A scream looks like it's going to escape her lips. My body tenses and waits for her saliva to shotgun across my face, but none ever arrives.

'And why is that?' Her voice is drenched in disappointment. I wish she'd have shouted at me instead.

‘B-because you c-can’t, and anyway there’s no room... It's my Papa that works at the factory. My Mama or my Babushka, erm, they’re n-not interested, they’d well- y’know - and I bet your family is the same. If all the girls in the world went to space, there would be nobody to raise children, or make amazing things like erm, pelmeni, because erm, my Papa can’t cook - he’s terrible y’know?’

I can feel my face going all red. After falling over my words so badly, part of me hopes she won't understand anything I've just said, and that she can just go back to staring at me from across the room or pretending to look at the sky when I come closer. Suddenly, in this moment, I miss her doing all that. If I could rewind time to about 35 seconds ago, I’d do it in a heartbeat.

Her hand turns into a tight fist, water beginning to form in her eyes.

‘I thought that you were different Yuri,’ she grabs Katarina’s hand and runs off towards the wall that Alikhan had disappeared behind earlier, probably with the same goal. Dimitri looks the happiest I’ve ever seen him. Nastya stops and turns when she’s halfway across the playground, making sure everyone can hear her next words.

‘Never talk to me again,’ she yells, tears starting to fall down her cheeks. She turns around and drags her friend away. Katarina looks as though she never wanted to leave in the first place but does so in support. Before I can mentally calculate what's going on, Marlen slaps me around the back of the head, his silver ring catching a tuft of my hair.

'What did you do? I was actually getting somewhere for once,' he's annoyed too, but for completely different reasons. I think he understands as much as me about what I didn't do wrong. I just didn't want her to get her hopes up. Girls stay at home, that's just the way it is. That's the way it's always been, right?

***

Nastya hasn't spoken to me since the incident on our first break. Marlen had tried to drag me over again to talk to the girls but they'd told him it was them or me. Inevitably, I was the one who ended up being told to leave. He says it's not personal, but it sure feels like it. Another example of girls becoming an integral part of Marlen's existence.

After that, I'd decided to spend my lunch break lying on the grass in the cold wind. The turf is dewy, and the sky is cloudy, all the ice from yesterday seems to have vanished. In my boredom I'm trying to make out pictures in the clouds. I can make out a bench with two people on it, one that looks like a long and pointy spear, and another that looks like the bird with a massive, coloured beak, with a name I can't remember without a textbook. Every now and then, the clouds break, and the sun touches my face for a few seconds, warming my cheeks before it's covered by grey again, causing my body to seize up until the next shine of light comes.

I can see Alikhan watching me from behind the wall he's claimed as his own. He looks like he wants to come over and chat, but I hope that he doesn't. No offence to him, but I'm just not in the mood to talk to anyone. Maybe he's watching because I don't mind being on my own. To be honest, I enjoy watching the clouds, wondering what everything would look like if I could ride one through the sky without falling through. It would be like being on the back of a dragon, like the stories they tell of the Zilant[14] in Kazan to the east. Babushka told me about them many moons ago, apparently, they have dragon heads, the legs of a chicken, the tail of a snake and dog ears. She says that in Kazan they always look into the sky, watching for big red wings to appear. Babushka has lots of great stories, I could sit and listen to her all day. My mind wanders to having my own cloud dragon. How amazing it would be to fly around the peaks of the Ural Mountains, catching my reflection in the big lakes below.

Alikhan's still watching me from across the playground. He seems so uncomfortable in his own head. It's nice being on your own sometimes, nobody interrupts you, or tries to correct you, or pushes you

---

14 A legendary creature hailing from Kazan.

out of bed because you're breathing too loudly, or abandons you to talk to girls, or screams in your face. In your own head you've got all the space in the world, to think about all the space outside of it.

I've always felt so comfortable in my thoughts, which makes sense, Babushka does call me Mechtatel after all. It would be silly to have a nickname that doesn't make any sense, like fish, or bin, or eggs and jam.

Mrs. Palakova interrupts my thoughts by ringing the bell for final class. I pick myself up from the grass, the mud under it stains the pants of my uniform. Mama would normally go crazy, but because it's a Friday and I don't need them tomorrow, I don't think she'll mind. I walk over to the line for my class, standing behind Alikhan who'd wandered over before me. He turns around like he wants to say something but stops himself; instead turning back around and waiting to go inside.

I'm still not in the mood to talk, so I leave it. My goal is to stay as silent as possible for the rest of the day, mostly in fear of offending anybody else. I'll make it up to everyone at the party, especially Nastya. I just don't want to be here anymore.

***

I sit and watch as Mikhail shuffles in his seat, he looks over his shoulder occasionally to try and catch

Dimitri's eyeline. It's just me, him and some other kids I don't really talk to at the table.

I just want to go home and paint my rocket for the flight tomorrow. I'm not in the mood for this, or to meet a new kid and his parents after school tonight. I watch as Mrs. Palakova walks around the classroom, checking up on my classmates and asking if they need any help. She's probably my favourite teacher at school, especially compared to the one we had last year, Mr. Dragunov. He's got a big scary moustache and enjoys shouting at the smallest sound from any of us. We'd spent that year in almost complete silence. He'd say that's how the country wants us to work in the future so it's good training for us. Mrs. Palakova is different though, she lets us chat and draw and be creative with our learning. It's taken her a while to pull us all out of our shells, an after-effect of Mr. Dragunov and his militant ways of *learning*. It's strange though, whenever another teacher comes in she barks at us to be quiet, almost like she's trying to hide what we're doing.

I watch as she bends over to talk to Katarina and Gertruda about the mitochondria. They're struggling to grasp that it's the powerhouse of the cell and that it controls everything else around it. In a way, our teacher is the mitochondria of the classroom, that's probably a good way to get them to understand it. I look back to Mikhail who'd caught me staring at our teacher, he pulls a stupid face that's similiar to the hyena in our textbook.

The look triggers something in my brain, and without thinking I flick back through the pages until I find the one I'm looking for. Scanning the text, I find the word I couldn't pull from memory yesterday, 'symbiotic'. Next to it is a picture of a hippopotamus and a bird eating the bugs off its back. I glance back up at Mikhail, I bet he eats bugs off Dimitri's back too.

I'll never understand why Mikhail doesn't get picked on like everyone else. How he's hidden underneath Dimitri's nose for so long without receiving a battering makes little sense to anyone. Maybe he's got a big scary brother or a Papa that would protect him if he even tried it, maybe his Mama makes Dimitri borscht[15] and his way of saying thanks is to not beat him to a pulp. He raises an eyebrow at me while I study his face. All he does is listen, if there's one person in the world that could probably braintalk outside of me and Mishka, my money is on him. He'd probably only learn how to do it so he can be nosey about what's going on.

'Turn around, mu-dak,' I almost brain-shout in his direction. I feel stupid, until he does. My face falls into shock at the fact I may have been right all along.

A hand touches my shoulder suddenly, causing ice to shoot up my spine. I've been lost in my

---

15 Sour soup made from beetroot.

thoughts again, like Babushka always tells me. I turn around, it's Mrs. Palakova. Mikhail sniggers to himself again.

'How are you finding the work, Yuri?' She says, looking at my workbook. I've barely written anything down, too busy thinking about my letter and the stupid wrinkly prune that is Mikhail's face. I look from the teacher, to my book, to the teacher again and force a laugh.

'I do understand it, I know the mitochondria runs the cell, just like you run the classroom.'

She giggles lightly to herself, 'too busy running around in your own thoughts again, Yuri? The mitochondria is what powers the cell, gives it energy,' she points at the lights on the ceiling of our classroom.

'That's your mitochondria right there, without that none of us would be here. If you wanted to think of us as the cell, I guess you could call me the nucleus, our classroom as the membrane that keeps everyone together, and all of the students are the cytoplasm.'

She bangs the desk with her fist slightly, 'and I guess you could call this the ribosome, it's a structure at least. Does that make more sense?' She smiles a mother's smile. I can't help but smile back.

'Yeah, I think so, I think I just prefer physics.'

'Just like your papa?'

'I guess so,' even though I agreed with her, I'm not sure what radios have to do with physics.

She smiles again and turns to walk away to a raised hand at the other side of the classroom.

'Uh, Miss?' I squeak.

'Yes, Yuri?'

'If I wanted to send a letter to the people in charge about something important, would you have their address?' I offer my pen to her confused expression.

'The people in charge? Of the school? Are you not enjoying your education, Yuri?' She places her hands on her hips, her blonde hair falling down her front.

'No. No. Sorry. No. The country, it's really important,' I'm scrambling my words, I don't want anything to happen to her, Mr. Dragunov yes, but Mrs. Palakova no.

'Oh, okay, you want the address… of the government?' She crouches down to the level of my desk, 'that hasn't got anything to do with biology, has it?'

She isn't wrong.

'I'll get you the address for your letter when class is over.'

'Miss! Miss!' Another child shouts from across the room loudly.

'I'll be there in a moment, there was another hand first. And what have we said about shouting instead of raising hands?'

She smiles and starts walking back towards the student who had their hand up first, she turns back to me as she walks.

'Do your *biology* work Master Rubinov, or I'll have to tell your parents you've been daydreaming again.'

My eyes widen and I start scribbling into my workbook about the cell of a plant. I can feel Mikhail's eyes burning into the top of my head as he stares, he's definitely been listening again. I wonder if his parents call him slushatel[16] at their house, because I swear it's all he ever does.

***

'Okay, that's it children, 3PM. Time to go, get home safe and enjoy your weekends. I'll see you all on Monday morning,' Mrs. Palakova has barely spoken her last words before all the other kids jump to their feet, pushing their belongings into their bags to run out of the door as fast as humanly possible.

'Oh, and happy birthday for tomorrow Gertruda!' She says quickly before the birthday girl leaves. Gertuda smiles and gives her a wave before leaving for the day.

---

16 Listener.

As Mrs. Palakova turns back to look at the remaining students in our classroom, I can see the pain on her face as Marlen screws up the piece of paper with all of his notes on into a ball, before throwing it into his bag, no doubt never to be read again. I take my time packing up my desk, it's not like I need to meet Vitor straight away, he's always ten minutes later than I finish so I normally have to wait in the playground for him anyway. Strangely, Mikhail's packing up slowly too, not chasing Dimitri out of the door like he normally does. What a little rat. Everything he does is so annoying. Why won't he just leave me alone?

'Dimitri's already left Mikhail, shouldn't you be running after him?' I tease.

He laughs, 'why are you in such a rush for me to leave?'

It's just me, him and Mrs. Palakova in the classroom now. I grab my bag and walk over to her, Mikhail sits at his desk pretending he isn't there.

'Hi,' I say to her, but her eyes are fixated on Mikhail, who's making it obvious he's lingering to be nosy.

'Mikhail Vasilyev, do you have any reason to be hanging around?' She asks him with a very serious tone. His face turns a bright raspberry red. A few words splutter incomprehensibly from his mouth, before he scrambles his things together and runs out of the doorway like the foaming dog near my house is chasing him.

My head turns back to Mrs. Palakova, she's holding out a piece of torn paper.

'Take it, I need to go home too,' I politely take it from her hands, reading her untidy and scribbled pencil lines before it leaves them.

First Secretary Khrushchev
Tsentrosoyuz Building
Moscow
Soviet Union, 101000

I don't try to hide the smile from my face.

'Thank you so much, Mrs. Palakova,' I can't help but jump up and down on the spot.

'Why do you need to send a letter to the government anyway?' She asks.

I look around for Mikhail, or anybody else, thankfully finding the coast clear. The classroom is completely empty, bar me and Mrs. Palakova.

'I'm going to space Miss, on my rocket at home. I want to let them know what it's like,' I can feel my face go warm, it feels more than strange to say it out loud.

She gives me a kind look and stands to her feet, rustling my hair with a gentle hand. People seem to do that to me all of the time, either I'm acting silly, or they think I'm cute, like some sort of puppy. I'm not sure I'm happy with either.

'Sounds like that's very important little one, why are you still here with such a key mission waiting for you at home?'

She's right. I have to go.

'Bye Miss, have a nice weekend!' I run out of the room as fast as I can, the open classroom door a goal for me to speed through. I get outside and turn left to exit the school grounds, before my chest sinks like it's full of lead. It's Mikhail, he's been standing outside listening to everything. Stupid little slushatel. He peers at the note I'm clutching in my hand, like it's his business to know what it says.

'Wait until Dimitri hears about this,' he says, reaching out to snatch the note from my hand. I pull away, clutching the paper tightly and running for the doorway. I can hear the squeaking of his shoes behind me on the hard floor, I burst through and kick the door closed. I watch as the door slams over Mikhail's irritating face, causing it to become shockingly even more rat-like.

I turn my head forward to run down the steps but collide into something tall and strong, I can't help but crash to the ground onto my elbows. I glance up to see the glare of Mr. Dragunov. My blood turns to ice, he doesn't even bother to look sorry or offer me a hand. All I can see from the floor is the long, black, bushy hair that sprouts from his nose and into his thick moustache. He coughs slightly into a loose fist, his eyes deadset into mine, like he's staring at something behind my head and I'm in the way.

'Attention soldier,' he barks, gesturing at me to stand up at attention with his hand.

'Rubinov, you're in Palakova's class. Where is she?' He snaps like the military officers on the radio. I scramble to my feet and salute him, like he makes us all do, even the girls.

'Mr. Dragunov, Sir, she's in our classroom,' my arm shakes as I hold it to my head, my elbow sore after its collision with the concrete.

'Very well. Go and have your weekend, child,' Mr. Dragunov keeps his serious face as he forces his way through the door and steps through. There are rumours around school that he's secretly KGB, keeping an eye on things at the school. I wonder why he wants Mrs. Palakova...

'Vasilyev…' I hear him bark, jogging my memory that Mikhail is right behind me. I resume my run towards the front gate, not stopping until I cross the playground. When I get there, I'm surprised to see Mama and Vitor standing together, chatting to somebody my height with their back to me. It's not like Mama to be here, normally it's just Vitor that walks me home. I look down the road as Polina and Nastya stroll home in the distance. A strange twinge pulls at my heart as I watch her walk away.

‘Good afternoon, Mechtatel,’ Mama says to me, ‘I didn’t know our dinner guest was in your class?’ My eyes snap from Nastya to Mama as though they’re made of elastic.

‘They are?’ I watch the boy's head turn.

‘Hi Yuri, who’s Mechtatel?’

A sigh escapes my lips. Not Alikhan.

***

I’m sitting in my living room, watching while Alikhan inspects my spaceship on the floor - he stares at the different tins of paint keenly. You can just tell he’s excited to get started on painting when our papas get here. Not to be mean, but I'd rather he just went home, surely his mama is there to look after him.

‘Your spaceship is so cool, Yuri. I’m so jealous that your parents let you do stuff like this. I’m hoping after my papa helps with yours, he’ll help me build one too,’ he runs his finger across the top box and down to the glued-on wing.

‘Be careful, just don't break anything,’ I tell him, my voice is more annoyed than I wanted it to be, he frowns slightly.

‘Have I upset you?’

‘No,’ my reply blurts out a lot faster than I thought it would.

‘Then why are you being so mean?’

‘I’m not.’

'You've not moved from your couch since we got here,' Alikhan plays with the skin on his arm, trying his hardest not to look at me.

'I...' I can't think of anything. He's right, I pull myself up off the couch and sit next to him alongside the rocket.

'Sorry.'

Alikhan shuffles in his place awkwardly, obviously not expecting his words to actually work.

'Why does your family call you Mechtatel?' He asks politely, no longer gawking at my spaceship, but at me instead.

'They say I space out a lot. I just like to think about things.'

'I've noticed you always seem to be looking around into the sky a lot at school,' he laughs. I don't. I'm not going to pretend that I didn't see him spying on me today. His laugh ends the moment he notices I'm not joining in. His eyes run around my living room again, obviously searching for something else to say.

'How come you decided to build the spaceship?'

'It's top secret,' he can ask me as many questions as he likes, he's not getting this out of me. Too many people already know and I already upset Nastya today by saying too much.

'Really?' Alikhan shuffles over to me with confidence, leaning into my ear and whispering quietly. The stench of the cottage cheese bake we had for lunch wafts into my face, making me wince slightly, 'sounds like you know about the Sputnik 1 project.'

I can't stop my mouth from falling to the floor. How does he know? Has Papa told him? It's then that I realise. It all makes so much sense. I look into his eyes.

'Sputnik's being launched from the Kazakh SSR, that's where your family is from! What do you know about it?' As soon as the words leave my mouth, Alikhan jumps at me and covers my mouth with his clammy hand. I struggle, but he holds me in place without much difficulty; he's actually much stronger than he looks. This would be so embarrassing if anyone from school saw us.

'You have to whisper. I'm going to tell you something crazy, but you can't tell anyone. Can I trust you?'

His words are relaxing, so I stop struggling. I lay there with his hand over my mouth, trying to nod as much as I can in his chokehold. A cough escapes my lips, covering his hand with slobber.

'Ew!' He throws me off, wiping his hand all over his school pants.

'Hey, you're the one with the sweaty hand and the smelly breath. I should be saying *ew* to you!' I snap back.

Alikhan folds his arms like he's cross, turning his head slightly away from me and breathing into his palm to see if I'm right. His face scrunches at what he finds, before settling into a sulk.

Ugh.

'Sorry, please tell me. I'll tell you what I know,' I try to pretend that I'm begging, but I'm definitely not pretending. This is everything I've ever wanted... since three days ago at least.

He shuffles forward on his knees, his school pants rubbing on the carpet uncovered by newspaper. He places a hand on my arm again, causing a static shock to travel between the two of us. He jolts back, like an explosion has gone off in my living room.

'Ah, sorry!'

I open my eyes wider, 'spit it out, Alikhan!'

He jolts again, this time without any static to cause it.

'W… well… my papa worked on the project, that's how your papa knows. They transferred him here to help at the facility to work on something else because they're just waiting to launch it. He knows *everything* about the *satellite.* He says that they're launching it from a place called Baikonur one fifth near Tyuratam next week, where I grew up, and that Uncle Sam's going to be *so* jealous.'

There's that Uncle Sam again, why is he so against everyone launching anything into space? I wonder if he's still sweating. Surely not consistently for this long? I've never heard of a place with a fraction in the name too, it sounds so science-y. I shake my head, getting rid of all these stupid thoughts. This is exciting, and to think I thought Alikhan was just some chudak from somewhere else in the Union. He might just be my winning ticket to space. I'm not quite sure what the word satellite means, but it's probably just another word for spaceship or rocket. A special Sputnik 1 word.

'D-do you think he'll answer questions about it?' I ask tentatively.

Alikhan shakes his head from side to side vigorously.

'He's sworn to secrecy, I'm surprised he told your papa really,' my heart sinks like a leaky boat, slowly and painfully. Looks like he isn't a winning ticket after all, but he may be helpful getting onto Sputnik 1 itself.

'Your secret is safe with me... well... it would have been.' I stutter over my words. Mikhail knows parts of my plan, but fortunately nothing about the Sputnik 1 project itself. Sure, I've told Nastya, Marlen and Mrs. Palakova and the whole of my family know about the rocketship in the front room, but they're trustworthy. Mikhail on the other hand is a complete sewer rat.

'What do you mean?' Alikhan asks, playing with the skin on his arm again.

I pull the crumpled-up note of paper from my pocket and show him the address. He looks at it curiously, his face telling me he's not putting the pieces together.

'That's the government's address, after my first flight into space I'm going to send them a letter. I want to be the first person in space. But when I was getting the address from Mrs. Palakova, Mikhail listened in through the doorway without me knowing. He knows about the spaceship,' I look over my shoulder towards my half-painted masterpiece.

'But he doesn't know about the *actual* Sputnik 1 project?'

'All he knows is I have the address of the government, that I've got a rocket at home and that I'm going to space. He's definitely going to tell Dimitri too, he probably already knows by now,' I hold my head in my hands, this is all making me feel so stressed.

Alikhan seems to relax, the panic from his eyes disappearing like all of this isn't a problem. Mikhail knows about the spaceship, it's only a matter of time until he finds out about Sputnik 1. This is catastrophic, why is Alikhan so calm? He's freaking me out. I run my hands through my hair, trying my best to scratch the itch on my aching brain. Alikhan places a comforting arm on my shoulder.

'Hey, just because he knows about it doesn't mean he can make his own,' the Kazakh boy smiles warmly at me, he's relaxed, so I should be relaxed too. I'm sure it's fine.

'So, what do you think we do?' I ask him, these are the sort of questions I normally ask Mishka, but I feel at ease with Alikhan. He's listening to what I have to say, which is more than my *best friend* Marlen has ever done. My brain wanders to him dragging me over to the girls, even after I told him I didn't want to.

'Hmm… maybe we could play one big joke on him, so he looks like a crazy person,' Alikhan blurts out in his Kazakh accent, his words linger in the air for a few moments as I let them sink in.

'And how would we do that?' I ask.

Alikhan crinkles the newspaper on the floor as he crawls over on his knees again, whispering his plan to me. His lips are close enough to my ear that the slobber that spits out tickles, making me laugh. It gets too much, forcing me to move away before I pull myself back together and let him carry on. His plan is brilliant, so simple, yet meticulous and will hopefully take down Dimitri and Mikhail once and for all.

Our conversation is interrupted by the front door opening, followed by two men that walk through laughing. One's obviously Papa, and after watching the way Alikhan jumps to his feet, the other man must be his. We run into the other room and greet them. Alikhan's papa is holding a bottle of something that my parents' like to drink occasionally. They're wearing the same uniform with the same white hat. I reach to grab it from Papa's head like I usually do, to get Poschekotat' Ruku to come out and play, but Papa swats my hand away gently.

'Not today Mechtatel, we've got company.'

'Hey Yuri, I've heard a lot about you! From Alexei and Alikhan,' he rubs his son's back before stretching out a hand to me. Why does everyone talk about me when they're at home?

'The name's Sanzhar,' he offers his hand, so I take it softly and shake it. Before I can say anything else, Babushka and Mama walk in and start introducing themselves. He hands the bottle to Mama as they invite Sanzhar through to the kitchen. Alikhan follows him, leaving me and Papa alone in the doorway.

He goes to follow everyone else, but I grab his white trouser leg, causing him to stop. He turns around and kneels down to the same level as me.

'Something the matter?' He asks, there's hair growing on his face that wasn't there yesterday.

'Where's his mama?' I ask, Papa's eyes drop as he glances into the other room, almost worrying that I said something too loudly.

'Erm… she's not with them anymore, little man. It's just the two of them. I don't know what happened, I haven't asked. Can you do me a big favour?' He nudges my chin with his hand.

'What's that?' I answer.

'Don't ask little Alikhan about it, it might upset him, you know?'

‘Ok, Papa.’

‘Promise?’

‘I promise.’

‘Then let's go and have some grub before everyone else eats it all,’ and with that, he grabs me with both hands, lifts me up and tickles me in mid-air causing me to laugh. He carries me towards the kitchen before turning back and shouting through our apartment.

‘Vitor, dinner!’

I hear a grunt, then the sound of heavy footsteps as he marches out of our bedroom.

***

I sit down in my chair and let the smell of beef stroganoff explore my nostrils. As we’ve got guests, it seems like Mama and Babushka have put more effort into cooking than usual. That’s not saying their normal cooking is bad, not at all, this just looks and smells like the best stroganoff they’ve ever made. They look so proud of their work as the steam floats up to kiss the ceiling. I glance over at Alikhan, his mouth is watering. Sanzhar looks the same now I notice it, his big bushy moustache is doing a terrible job of hiding the smile from his lips. They both look very excited to eat. So does Papa. Vitor just looks like Vitor. Miserable, like someone has smacked him in the face with a pan.

We're all sitting around a large stewing pot in the middle of the table, a steaming bowl of rice sits next to it with a large spoon poking out, just waiting to be served. My stomach growls like it hasn't been fed in days. Papa says the rest of the country doesn't get to eat as much as we do, but that doesn't sound fair. We aren't greedy, if they have less food than we do then everyone would starve, so I don't think he's telling the truth, he probably just wants me to eat my peas.

Everyone around the table has started conversations I'm not interested in; I'm too focussed on the stroganoff at the centre of the table.

'So, how's work going with you two?' Mama asks, Papa opens his mouth to answer but Sanzhar beats him to it.

'We really can't say, it's top secret after all, and anyway, it's far too advanced of a conversation for women and children to be having,' he scratches his wide chin with a smug look, 'may I say that your stroganoff looks delightful.'

I catch Alikhan's eyes, if it's that top secret why do we know what's going on with Sputnik 1. If anything, my rocket in the living room is more advanced than the radios he's making at work.

Mama smiles differently than normal, almost straining to get it out. The kind eyes that normally settle into her face as she smiles aren't there - instead it's the body language she has when me and Vitor are fighting, only the rest of her face doesn't match. I wonder whether anyone else notices what's going on with her. Papa's leaning back in his chair, peering past Sanzhar, like he's trying to get Mama's attention. If he is, she's refusing to look. Papa looks like a worm trapped in a glass jar. The table has fallen into silence. Babushka reaches over to the rice and grabs the spoon, the movement causes the fluffy rice to breathe steam into the air again.

'Alright, who's hungry?' Babushka says, grabbing Sanzhar's plate and shovelling on an overflowing spoon. Everyone starts talking again, except for Mama, she's just staring at her empty plate.

'What are you going to name your spaceship, Yuri?' Sanzhar suddenly asks me, rice sticking to his hairy upper lip like white maggots. I look from him, to Mama and back again.

'I really can't say, it's top secret after all, too advanced for *you* to understand.'

Mama's face changes again as the softness returns to her eyes, Papa covers his mouth with his hand. Sanzhar turns to him, as if to question what I'd said.

Vitor's sitting to my left, he stretches a fist towards me as Sanzhar isn't looking, for once he isn't punching me, but waiting for me to tap my knuckles into his, which I do excitingly.

He winks and smiles at me for the first time in a long time.

'Nice one, little bro,' he whispers.

I look back up at Papa and Sanzhar, Papa's telling him that kids will be kids. Sanzhar's going on about children not being so rude in the Kazakh SSR. Alikhan's just eating his stroganoff in silence, that seems like the best thing to do, so I do the same. I shovel a mouthful of creamy beef and rice into my mouth and chew slowly, the taste is amazing. I look back at Mama who's now chatting away happily with Babushka while she eats, food tastes better when she's happy.

***

Sanzhar and Alikhan decided to go home early, telling us that they'll be listening to the radio at home instead of with us. It's sad because in the end I actually wanted Alikhan to stay and help me name my spaceship, but now he's gone. He said that he'll definitely be at Gertruda's birthday party tomorrow though. I'm looking forward to seeing him again, our plan together will be great. Dimitri and Mikhail have no idea what's coming for them.

Babushka's pottering around the kitchen tidying up all the mess, she'd told Mama that she'll be the one to clean up because Mama had done most of the cooking. I can hear her wretched cough from this room, it's the kind that sounds like a chunk of you is going to come flying out, or at least something thick and gooey. She always sniffs loudly afterwards too, like she's trying to suck the gunk back in.

Mama's sitting listening to the radio, idly watching Papa and I paint. The song echoing around the room is some military one, with loud trumpets and drums. She turns down the knob and leans down to us painting on the floor, resting her elbows on her knees. Mama plants a kiss on my head, causing Papa to look at her enviously until she gives him one as well.

'Out of interest Mechtatel, what *will* you be calling your spaceship?' Mama's voice is soft, Papa raises his eyebrows at the question too.

'That's easy, Sputnik 0.5,' I carry on painting the cardboard of my ship bright red. Mama and Papa are quiet for a moment, before they both burst out laughing.

'Probably a good job you didn't tell Sanzhar!' Papa says, the wrinkles on his head deepen as he laughs. Whenever he's angry or sad, his face gets so crumpled. That's why he's got so many old lines. I start laughing with them both. Papa waits for me to finish painting the red and pulls over the yellow, yanking the lid off and covering the tips of his fingers with a thick coat of paint. He wipes them across my cheeks in chunky lines, I can't stop myself from smiling.

‘Dip a finger in Mechtatel, and you Mila, let’s write the name on.’ Papa uses his finger to wipe a streaky ‘S’ on the side, then Mama does the ‘P’.

‘Next is the ‘U’, little man.’

I nod and paint it on, it’s a lot messier than theirs. I turn back to look at them as Mama pokes Papa on the nose, painting it yellow. They then start play-fighting each other, getting paint all over their clothes. I decide to leave them to it and carry on the spelling, next up is a ‘T’ right?

I look towards the doorway before I paint it on, I can see Vitor watching us from the hallway. I point at the yellow tin and wave him over, but he just storms off into the kitchen without a word.

‘Hello there, Vitor,’ I hear Babushka say with the croak of an old frog, sounding like she still hasn’t got the goop out of her throat.

***

‘What do you mean the launch has to wait until tomorrow evening? We’ve got everything ready, it just needs to dry overnight and we can do it in the morning?’ Mishka’s beady eye stares right into my soul, he’s unhappy about me going to Gertruda’s party.

‘I wouldn’t mind, but I have to stay here and look at the wall. Your house is so boring when you’re not here, maybe I'll just launch Sputnik 0.5 by myself,' he'd fold his arms in protest if he could.

All I can do is laugh, 'you know you won't be able to do that, you don't even know how the controls work. You'll have all of our hard work crashed into the side of the Urals.'

'I'll just learn them while you're out, you'll see,' he retorts.

I laugh in braintalk, some of it slipping out of my lips.

'Shut up,' Vitor snaps with the force of a venus fly trap.

Mishka and I are hiding under our blankets so Vitor can't see us. The fabric stops us from being too loud and disturbing him, as well as acting as a cover for his snoring for when we finally decide to go to sleep. We wait for a minute, everything's quiet, then suddenly Vitor's bed creaks and I can hear footsteps storming towards us. The blanket comes flying off, suddenly I'm face-to-face with my brother. He stares me down like I'm some sort of unwanted animal that managed to find its way inside.

'What are you even doing? Why are you hiding?' He looks at Mishka with a confused *why are you with your bear, please don't tell me you still think you can talk to it* face.

'He's onto us,' Mishka squirms unmoving.

I can't do anything but stare at him blankly, not really sure what to say. The outline of his body becomes clearer the longer I look at him in the darkness, so do the angry creases on his face.

'Okay mu-dak. Don't say anything, I guess? I absolutely have no idea why Polina and Nastya are so nice to you, nevermind Babushka, Mama, and Papa. You do nothing but talk to your little bear and think to yourself. It's so weird, you're so weird,' Vitor scoffs in disbelief. He lets go of the blanket in midair, letting it float back down, covering me and Mishka untidily. I listen to his footsteps, then the squeak of springs as he throws himself back into bed. Then there's silence again, I don't even risk braintalking in case he can hear me.

Saturday 28th September, 1957.

City 40, Chelyabinsk Oblast, Russian SFSR, Soviet Union.

Today is definitely not the day for a birthday party. There's no sun for a start and there are clouds filling the sky as far as my eyes can see. The wind is blowing into my face as we walk up to Victory Square. It could be worse, it could be snowing like it was the other day.

Vitor and Babushka are walking up the road towards the big park just ahead, leaving me to struggle with carrying everything like a pack mule. In my hands is a backpack wrapped in brown paper that crinkles as I walk. When we were in the store, I wanted to get Gertruda a stuffed elephant around the same size as Mishka, but with two eyes of course. I'd spotted it on the shelf and in my head had already named it 'Artyom'. Babushka had swatted away the idea, and the elephant, almost immediately. She says that practical gifts are always the ones that are most appreciated, but I already don't believe her. Maybe someday I'll get to buy an Artyom for myself. Thinking of that makes me feel better.

The only reason Vitor's here is because Polina is coming with Nastya. I wonder where their parents are, I've never seen them or heard anybody talk about them. I look up at Babushka as she shuffles across the concrete, maybe some people think my parents don't exist either.

Vitor hasn't spoken to me since pulling the blanket off me last night, he hasn't even looked at me on our walk. I don't think I'll ever find out why he's always so angry with me. I'd probably talk to Mishka less if I could talk to him, but all he does is throw me out of bed when I breathe too loudly or storm off when I ask him to paint. I don't really know what he wants from me.

'Why she's having a party outdoors in September I'll never know,' Babushka grumbles, her skin obviously thinner than mine and Vitor's. Especially Vitor's now that I think about it.

The three of us turn right into the square, I look straight at the big statue that greets everybody who walks in. It looks like a person kneeling down with a giant metal sword and a baby sitting dangerously on their lap. I can't tell whether the statue is a man or a woman, or what the baby is either. All I know is that someday I'm going to take that sword home, and the next time Vitor's mean to me, I'll whack him out of the window with it.

Behind the statue, there are loads of pointy trees and a path going towards Lake Irtyash. I can see the handmade paper decorations hanging on the trees near the bottom, all in the shape of sunflowers. The sound of screaming children echoes down the path. I look up at Babushka, my feet bouncing on the floor without me noticing. I want to go over there now, why are they walking so slowly? The rucksack crinkles again in my hands, getting Babushka's attention, she looks at me and smiles.

'Go on then, we'll be right behind you.'

I don't need telling again. I start running towards the birthday party, tucking the bag under my arm as the statue and its baby watch me leave with their staring eyes. They look so serious, like they're warning me away. I feel strange as I jog behind it, away from its gaze and through the gate towards the party. The stony path makes it easy for my shoes to flick up little rocks, the dust painting my face. I can see my classmates starting to come into view; they're all wearing long pointy red hats made of paper. I watch as Katarina's bends in the wind like a falling tower, the crease in its side causing the top to smack into the side of her face. She struggles to straighten it, but once a birthday hat creases, it's impossible to set it right again, I thought everyone knew that.

I can see Marlen and Alikhan in a corner by themselves, the blond looking animated as the Kazakh tries his best to speak to him. On the other side of the party Dimitri, Mikhail, Katarina and Nastya are hanging out together. That last name feels so strange to list with the rest. Our disagreement still lingers in my mind like stubborn black ice on a warm day.

My sprint towards Alikhan stops when Gertruda's intimidating figure steps in my way, causing me to skid to a stop, coating her in a cloud of dust that sticks easily to her yellow, flowery dress. She doesn't look pleased to see me and frowns like Sanzhar had done at dinner last night. I look towards where the parents are standing, I can see him there, pulling the same face at me that he was last night. Gertruda fluffs her dress with her hands, causing a dusty cloud to float away like ash. I sneeze a little as it rises into my face.

'Sorry, Gertruda. Happy Birthday!' One of my eyes is still set on my friends talking, Marlen looks completely unamused. I hold out the wrapped-up rucksack with the hope that she takes it and leaves.

'Yuri! You've got dust all over my new dress,' she stamps the floor like a toddler, getting more dust on it, anyone would think that this is a baby's birthday party.

I shake the brown present in front of her eyes, which helps her forget pretty quickly about the dust I'd just sprayed all over her. She tears into it, like a bear hunting fresh salmon. Her happy face suddenly reverts back to annoyance; I knew that we should have bought her Artyom instead.

'A rucksack?' Her hands drop to her sides in frustration.

'*I* wanted to get you something else.'

'Then why didn't you?' Her hands squeeze so tightly that her knuckles start to whiten, the vein on her neck looks as though it's going to burst. How ungrateful is she? I know it isn't the greatest gift in the world, but she can at least pretend to like it. She's acting like I'm the one who earned the money, went out and bought it, in case she hasn't noticed I'm a kid too - we go to the same school. Oh no, her teeth are beginning to scrape together, she's going to blow. I brace for impact.

'Because you've had the same backpack for years, dear,' Babushka says, having finally caught up with me, half of me wishes that I'd never run off in the first place. Vitor walks straight over to Polina. Why does he get to go straight to where he needs to be? Why can't Gertruda have stopped him instead?

Gertruda's face changes immediately the moment Babushka arrives, like she'd been hiding a mask in her hands, placing it over her face when nobody was looking. Her change from angry fury to pleasant parental cuteness right in front of my eyes is jarring. I look down at her knuckles, they're still tense and white around the straps of the rucksack. I use the distraction as my moment to slip away.

'Oh yes! Thank you ever so much Mrs. Rubinov, I love it,' I watch her say through gritted teeth.

'Well, aren't you something,' Babushka says in return with a chuckle, before her wheezing cough echoes over the sound of everything else. Her distraction causes Alikhan and Marlen's conversation to stop with a jolt as I approach, giving me an opening to talk about *the plan.*

Marlen's eyes shoot to me immediately, 'so you're friends with the chudak now? How did this happen? You two have some sort of prank planned? I can't believe this.'

Alikhan's standing red-faced.

'Woah Marlen, stop being so mean,' I say sternly, his nostrils flare like an angry snake that's been disturbed in the grass.

'Mean? He's foreign. Why should we help him? He won't even tell me why this is so important,' his knuckles are pale like Gertruda's. Wait a minute, that's it.

'Marlen,' I place my hands on his shoulders, 'For one, Alikhan's from the Kazakh SSR. It's a part of the Union, he's not foreign. And the plan,' I look at

Alikhan and nod. Marlen looks at me curiously, briefly dropping his anger for interest.

'It's about the girls.'

Alikhan stands in dumbfounded silence as Marlen glances back at him, the Kazakh's face painted with visible confusion. My best friend turns back to me.

'What do you mean about the girls?'

'Aren't you sick of them hanging around with Dimitri and Mikhail?' I turn and point towards the five of them discreetly, Gertuda after her outburst has gone over and joined them. They're standing around chatting with their big pointy red hats on; Marlen follows my eyes, but his obviously set on Katarina.

'Yeah, I am.'

'What if we can stop that happening forever? I had a think about what you said yesterday, Marlen, I do care about girls. So does Alikhan.'

The Kazakh looks like he's going to fall over. He's a boy of science too, after all.

'Which one?' Marlen asks him sternly, his tone deadly serious.

'Uh…'

'Gertruda,' I say, 'he's just nervous.'

Marlen turns back to me, 'strange choice. But three of us, three of them I suppose. The math makes sense,' he pushes my hand off his shoulder.

‘Let’s get to it then, Katarina’s been looking at me all morning and I’ve been dying for a reason to go over. What's the plan?’

The three of us huddle together, so tightly that nobody else can hear what we’re saying.

***

‘Do you know how *stupid* you both sound?’ Marlen breaks out of our cluster with a shout, catching the attention of the rest of the party, ‘I can’t believe you’re trying to get me involved with this.’

He pushes us both away, causing me and Alikhan to fall to the ground with an *oof*. Dust floats up into the air; behind the cloud that appears I can see Gertruda smiling with the colour of revenge. Her mask has obviously fallen off already, her sour face the happiest I’ve seen it at her own birthday party. I look over at Nastya, it’s the first time she’s glanced in my direction since I’ve been here. She isn’t laughing like the others. The pain in my chest returns the more my eyes linger on her.

Marlen storms off toward them all, huffing as he goes. Alikhan looks at me with a painted face of panic. I allow my head to fall to the dirt, causing another slight dust cloud to blow up from my blond hair. I stare into the clouds, there are so many that they don’t resemble shapes at all, just a big grey pile of mush that floats through the air as fast as the wind can push it.

'Mechtatel, you're going to get your nice clothes all dirty. Get up!' Babushka hisses like the old lady she is. I dust myself off as she places one of the party hats on my head, the long and red point stretches up into the sky, like it's trying its best to mix the clouds together.

'I don't know what that was all about young man, but you'd better behave from this point on, or I'm taking you and your brother home.'

Vitor hears her statement and shouts over, 'that's not fair, why do I have to go home?'

All Babushka does is glare at him until he turns back around to Polina in silence, his eyebrows raised out of fear. She stomps off back towards the group of adults. I catch Sanzhar staring at me sternly, that man is so angry for no reason. I spot Vitor and Polina whispering behind the crowd of parents, before nodding to each other and slinking off behind one of the trees, most likely to touch noses again. Ugh, this is not the time.

My gaze falls to Marlen, he seems to be protesting with his hands, throwing them around in big circles yet speaking in hushed whispers. Every now and then, Dimitri and Mikhail look over at us, their ears still hooked on the words that leave Marlen's mouth. The girls have wandered off somewhere together, but that's fine, if anything it's better that way. My hand clutches at the piece of paper that's screwed up in my pocket.

'I can't tell what he's saying,' Alikhan has walked up behind me without me noticing, startling me out of my trance.

'Alikhan, you can't just sneak up on people like that!' I say, clutching my heart instinctively like it would have burst out of my chest otherwise.

'Sorry, but still, can you understand him?' He asks again awkwardly.

'No, but they keep looking over.'

'How do we know he's actually doing it? I can't read him very well. That exit was too convincing,' Alikhan squeezes his arm as he tries to calm himself. He isn't wrong to be wary of Marlen after how he's treated him, but he's forgetting the one thing he values more than anything else. Girls.

Dimitri jolts an angry finger into Marlen's chest as if on cue. His hands rise as the larger boy creeps into his personal space, I can only imagine the warm air from Dimitri's nostrils blasting across his face. I watch as words fall out of Marlen's mouth like dribble, his lips quivering, his eyes darting from Dimitri's intimidating form to us, then back to him, then to Mikhail, then back to us, and finally to the adults who watch over all of us so intently. It really is great acting, it's a shame that in school we have very little time to study drama. Marlen could easily work in theatre when he's older. He got sent home once because he faked a leg injury so well that he convinced Mrs. Palakova that he couldn't walk, going as far as to collapse on the grass when she told him to stand up straight. It didn't matter though, his mama sent him straight back the moment he got home. Mamas always know the truth.

The hand that prodded his chest turns into a palm that slowly pats Marlen, causing him to wobble, this show of friendship from Dimitri seemingly catching him more off-guard than the violent prodding of the finger beforehand. Mikhail's hands are folding in and out of each other as he stares over at me and Alikhan. The eyes of the beast turn to us, I force the crumpled paper into Alikhan's hands as the hulking Dimitri walks towards us with a smirk, the yappy Mikhail scurrying around his feet like a small and irritating puppy.

'It worked. Run!' I yelp at Alikhan, he doesn't need telling again, he hightails it towards a tree within the park to try and hide. Dimitri's course alters, seemingly aiming straight for the Kazakh. The large boy approaches him slowly, like a wild bear hunting its prey. That leaves me with…

'I'm onto you, Yuri,' Mikhail's voice hisses, 'you and your little spy friend, you're both going to be arrested and sent to the gulags. And your families. And your family's friends. Except for the girls, of course.'

I'm not sure he knows how the system works.

‘I have no idea what you’re talking about Mikhail.’

‘Yes you do, don’t act smart with me.’

‘I can’t help it.’

His face scowls, ‘I know you have the address of the government, I know he’s a spy, Marlen’s just told me that you and your family are plotting with his family to destroy the Union. We all know both of your papa’s work at Mayak. Don't deny it, it’ll just cause a scene. Dimitri is chasing down that little weasel now, he’ll find that note you just forced him to run away with. You can’t hide anything from me, Yuri, I'm far too clever.’

Mayak, I think to myself, not sure what the radio factory Papa and Sanzhar work at has to do with this.

My eyes dart to the tree that Alikhan had previously run off to, Dimitri walks out confidently, dragging the smaller Kazakh boy by his scrawny left leg. A baby blue sock is visible, his pale calf shining brighter than the overcast sky. Above Alikhan, a ball of dust circles, growing as Dimitri drags him across the ground, a scrunched up piece of paper flaps around his mouth with the wind, held on by Dimitri’s yellow teeth.

‘Hey, get your hands off my son,’ Sanzhar finally gets involved and begins storming over to us.

‘Get away from me, Kazakh spy,’ Dimitri spits venomously, causing the approaching Sanzhar to stop and turn to the adults at the party furiously.

'Who's child is this? He needs a good beating.'

Mikhail's frail mother stands silently in the crowd, she's the one watching them, as always. Yet as always, not a peep comes out of her; she just sips whatever's in her cup and watches on, seemingly more distracted by the clouds that float around in the sky or the waves that crawl gently onto the banks of the lake.

The silence does nothing but further infuriate Sanzhar, he turns back to Dimitri, seemingly ready to enact his own revenge. For a non-spy he's taking this very aggressively. You can tell all the adults at the party are starting to feel uncomfortable, yet none of them act, they just seem to be waiting for what's next or for a director to shout *'scene'* from behind a bush somewhere.

Mikhail pulls the note from Dimitri's mouth, like this has been some weird game of fetch, stopping Sanzhar dead in his tracks as he holds it up like a weapon.

'I have proof,' Mikhail says.

Sanzhar's eyes shoot to Alikhan viciously, before moving back to my enemy, Mikhail. The scrap paper crinkles loudly as it opens, the sound carried by the wind. Sanzhar looks like he's about to open his mouth, yet Mikhail beats him to it.

'Dimitri's going to read what it says,' he snivels, palming off the soggy note of paper back to his friend.

The bald boy shrugs and holds it in front of his face, his eyes focusing as his mouth opens.

'The secret plans of Alikhan and Yuri,' he bellows proudly, as though he doesn't already have the attention of the entire party. Sanzhar's eyebrows furrow confusedly. He shoots a look at Babushka, then Vitor, seemingly having returned from his trip with Polina, then to me.

'Is to send the government of the Soviet Union, a letter, with the sole aim of - aim of…' Dimitri stutters, looking towards Mikhail for help.

'Read it, kid!' Vitor shouts. He almost sounds interested in what the note says.

'Aim of, proving that Dimitri and Mikhail are fools who know nothing, and they deserve to be thrown in the gulag for... for...'

'For what mu-dak?' Vitor interrupts again, with half a smile this time. Polina smacks his chest, causing him to retreat awkwardly.

'For their… stupidity,' Dimitri utters defeatedly.

'What?!' Mikhail stomps over to him, snatching the note from his hands and quickly scurrying across it with his spider eyes, his face turning more tomato-like as he does so. Sanzhar erupts into a bellowing laugh that all the adults begin to follow, guided by the Kazakh pied piper. I watch Sanzhar closely, a bead of sweat races down his face, falling off and staining the white dust of the ground below. His laugh bounds around Victory Square, as his eyes dart around it, catching the face of Alikhan with a subtle but unmissable glare. Yet when he looks away from his son the happiness returns, a genuine smile hiding in plain sight across his face. I glance toward his hands, the veins on them still straining, bulging as though they're going to pop. They're worse than Gertruda's were when we spoke before, like he too has an elaborate mask covering his true feelings. I catch a look at Alikhan, he's playing with the skin on his arm like he normally is, avoiding looking anyone directly in the eyes.

'Kids will be kids, I suppose. I think they're just built differently here to what I'm used to,' Sanzhar scratches the back of his neck, leaving a couple of red lines trailing behind his fingernails.

'But, but…' Mikhail splutters, 'I heard you talking to Mrs. Palakova about the rocket.'

'Haha, you mean that cardboard box in the front room?' Babushka says, 'that thing couldn't even make it out of the door without falling apart.'

The adults settle into a more natural laugh at the expense of Dimitri and Mikhail, as well as the Sputnik 0.5 project in my front room. They're all laughing at my rocket, but I'll show them, they don't know what its true power is. Maybe it's for the best that they laugh, this is a top-secret mission after all. I bite my tongue and let them all have their moment. They'll see, they'll all see.

Dimitri looks over to me, placing a finger to his neck and swiping across it before he and Mikhail run off towards the latter's mother, who's still interested in everything but them, not that I can blame her. I watch as they beg to be taken home. Monday probably isn't going to be the most fun day at school, but it's worth it to teach them a lesson, and to keep the Sputnik 1 project a secret.

The adults go back to their conversations, some of them still laughing, Sanzhar still sweating like he's actually got something to hide.

'How good was I?' Marlen punches me in the arm as he walks over, before doing the same to Alikhan and shooting him a smile. Maybe there's hope for them both being friends after all.

'Really good, I thought you'd actually turned on us,' Alikhan laughs gently, rubbing the area of his arm that had been on the receiving end of Marlen's punch.

'Letting him drag you out like that as well Alikhan, it was genius, it got everybody's attention,' the blond Russian slaps the back of the Kazakh, who giggles nervously.

'Yeah, totally…'

I look forward and notice Gertruda and Katarina walking toward us. I search around for Nastya, almost by complete instinct, but she's already gone. Vitor's standing on his own, half-listening to a conversation that Babushka's half-listening to herself. It seems I'm going to have to wait until Monday until I get to talk to Nastya. My stomach drops, Monday's shaping up to be an awful day, part of me hopes it never arrives.

'Hey ladies, did you catch all that?' Marlen slicks back his hair with his own saliva, I watch as it sticks the loose ends of it back easily. I'll have to remember that.

'Yeah, how crazy were those two acting?' Katarina replies.

'Are you feeling okay, that looked like it hurt?' Gertruda asks Alikhan, somewhat sincerely for her. He starts burning a bright red.

'Yeah, much better,' he smiles genuinely, almost as if he's starting to believe that this was for her attention as well.

'You know what Yuri, I can see them together,' Marlen smiles at me, before Alikhan returns a hard dig into his arm, causing him to yap. Getruda and Katarina laugh gently with my two friends. It's quite a cute moment really, I just wish Nastya was here too.

I look over towards Vitor, who's laughing at one of the adult's jokes, I catch a glint of his teeth through his smile. It's so strange seeing him this way, he's normally so sour, like his blood is made of lemon juice, always intent on ruining my day for his own enjoyment. After he sees Polina though, he acts like it's our birthday truce all the time, where he isn't allowed to wind me up or pick on me. It's what he gets me every year instead of a present. Surely it would be less effort to just leave me alone all year.

Around Polina though, Vitor always has a smile on his face, one that sticks around for a time after she leaves. I wonder if he can tell her from a row of girls standing facing the other way like I can with Nastya, maybe we aren't so different after all? He catches my eye and the smile disappears, replaced with the normal look he glares at me with. Maybe not then.

***

It's finally time. Mishka and I are in the bathroom making our final arrangements before we take flight. Our spaceship, Sputnik 0.5, is waiting in the living room. This is going to be a long journey and one that we won't be back from for some time. I put my head beneath the tap and slurp from the water that dribbles out, making sure to catch each tasty droplet. I turn to Mishka and wipe my hand across my mouth, focusing on his gross and matted face.

'Are you ready?' I braintalk my thoughts to him.

'Ready when you are,' his voice is hoarse. I hope he slept well last night.

'Then let's go,' I lift up the box next to me, it has two eyeholes cut out of it, and is just big enough to fit over my head. I can barely make out the room with the small eyeholes, but with space equipment you have to sacrifice comfort for breathing. I pick up the smaller box from the side, sliding it over Mishka's head. I only made one eyehole in Mishka's box; he doesn't need the other after all. I lift up Mishka and leave the bathroom, intense music pounds in my head as we walk towards our launch pad. I can hear Mishka's heartbeat, and the chopping of carrots from the kitchen. I ignore the chopping sounds; they're not cool enough for a moment like this. Looking down at Mishka, I can tell he's just as nervous as me. This is it.

We approach our cardboard machine; the blue and red paint job makes it stand out in our boring living room. The *Sputnik 0.5* Mama, Papa and I had painted on, shines brightly in yellow. I open the lid of the rocket and place Mishka at the back of the spaceship with my hand. I turn back to my living room, taking it all in, not knowing when I might see it again. I salute the room like we do to the Union flag at school before I turn back to the rocket.

I follow Mishka through the hatch at the top, squeezing myself into our ship and letting it fall behind me. The slit from the opening rests on my head, keeping it from falling through completely. I reach up and turn the key to the lock, making it click into place. Now that we're safely inside, I remove my helmet and look forward out of the window, towards the fields and mountains that surround City 40. The Urals in the distance look like the only thing between us and the rest of the universe. As the sun sets, it makes the field in front of our runway an orangey-green. I take a slow deep breath and grab the steering wheel; I turn to Mishka.

‘No turning back now. Are you ready?’

Mishka swivels in his chair to face me at the front, scribbling away into a notepad. He takes off his helmet to see more clearly, his beady eye inspecting the inside of Sputnik 0.5.

‘As ready as I’ll ever be,’ I can hear the fabric of his mouth moving freely, ‘thrusters are ready, we’re powering on. All you have to do is flick the switch.’

‘You really did learn the controls when I was out didn’t you?’

‘Bears don’t lie,’ he chuckles gruffly.

I grab the wheel as tightly as I can, my hands shaking.

‘Three…’

‘Two…’ Mishka says seriously, like he always does.

‘O-one…’ The last word struggles to leave my lips. I push the wheel forward with a jolt, creating a deafening explosion at the back of our spacecraft. It sounds like Papa’s car times a million, my eyes widen as Sputnik 0.5 bounds toward the mountains. I struggle to hold onto the wheel. Mishka isn’t making a sound, but he’s never the type to scream when he’s scared. I, on the other hand, absolutely am.

I can’t tell what’s louder, the rocket engine or my yelling. The wheels of our craft start bouncing up and down on the runway, eager to lift off. I pull back the steering wheel, our spaceship leaves the ground at an angle, with the buildings of City 40 behind us getting further and further away.

'We're off the ground!' I shout to Mishka. I turn to face him, he's as pale as a ghost.

'What's wrong?' I ask, before he points directly at the window without a word. I turn back around; we're flying straight into one of the mountains, it grows more and more large the longer we head in its direction.

'Ah!' I yell in panic, instinctively turning the steering wheel left with a jolt, sending our speeding rocket around the mountain and straight towards another.

'Yuri, there's more, turn right!' Mishka shouts, I do as I'm told without protest, yanking the wheel right as we dodge another mountain. In the distance, they get increasingly jagged and dangerous. It's a good job that we won't go anywhere near them. I pull back on the steering wheel again, sending us flying straight up into the air towards the sky. Darkness has started to fall on the city, so much so that the Moon is becoming visible. I use it as my guide and fly directly towards it.

'Mishka! Speed boost!'

'Yes sir!' His soft hand jams into a big red button at his desk, a loud clunk can be heard from the spaceship as it starts going faster and faster. We zoom towards the Moon like we're racing on sports day.

‘I think I’m gonna be sick!’ I yell, my stomach spinning.

‘You’d better not be!’ Mishka snaps back. To be fair, vomit would be a nightmare to get out of his fur. It’s already happened once, after Marlen’s birthday party a few years ago; I’d eaten too much cake. I came home to tell him all about it and couldn’t stop it from coming out. Following that, Mama hadn’t let me see Mishka for days, it was so lonely. He’d lost so much colour when he was finally returned to me, probably because he’d missed me too.

‘Yuri!’ I come back to my senses as Mishka shouts, ‘you’ve gone straight past the Moon!’

I look out of the side window as we speed past the big ball of goat’s cheese, little green people are jumping up and down on its surface. Mishka was right, I’d been so caught up in dreaming about Marlen’s birthday that I’d driven past the Moon, now we’re speeding into the darkness of space, further and further away from our intended target.

‘One second, let me turn this thing around,’ I yank the wheel to the left, sending Mishka flying into the wall of our spaceship.

‘Ouch,’ he slides down the glass window.

‘Sorr- wow…’ I forget everything that's going on, all my focus absorbed by the view of our planet. It’s massive and green and blue, and I can see all the white clouds floating over the surface.

'Look! I see Earth! It's so beautiful,' I say to Mishka, pointing at it from space, 'there's City 40 and the Urals. I wonder if Babushka, Mama, and Papa can see us!' I wave instinctively, before realising I'm probably a bit too far away for them to see my flailing hand. I look over the big colourful blob we call Earth, if I squint slightly I feel like I can see all the different countries I've learnt about at school, places like China, Brazil and America. I wonder if sweaty Uncle Sam is watching? I bet he's so jealous.

My vision falls back to City 40, then slightly further east, over to Kazan. I squint slightly, straining my eyes. I swear I can see bright red wings flying around. They disappear just as quickly as they appeared, vanishing without a trace. My brain buzzes around my head. Have I just seen a Zilant? Babushka is going to be so excited when I tell her.

My thoughts are stopped by a loud alarm that threatens to burst my ears into a million pieces. Our white control room turns a dark red. I can hear the alert sounding throughout the whole ship. Something is obviously wrong.

'Yuri, look!' Mishka points out of the front window with his furry hand, I can't believe what I'm seeing. There are four rocket ships in front of us, all metal and painted green. They're shaped like long cylinders with circle windows, inside of them little green people point at us like we're some sort of alien spaceship. The front one is bigger than the others, on its side in white paint it says 'Moon Force'. A green woman with a captain's hat stares at us angrily through the window. I notice that there's a long tube poking out from underneath their largest ship. While I watch it, it stretches through space to the underside of Sputnik 0.5. A noise echoes throughout our ship, above the alarms, almost sounding like Mama opening a tin of stewed pork. Our ship rumbles like an earthquake has hit. Mishka and I go flying into the rear wall as the entire ship tilts backwards. Sputnik 0.5 reluctantly heads toward the alien fleet. I can see their captain laughing through their weird windows.

'Not today!' I shout, 'Mishka, man the controls. We're not being made into alien borscht,' I pull myself across the floor of the ship. My sweaty, pruney fingers stick to the clean tiling as I drag my body towards the steering wheel, the clanging of metal is so loud that it can probably be heard on Earth. Sputnik 0.5 rumbles as it tears through space, creaking almost angrily at being diverted off-course.

'Aye aye, captain,' he salutes and starts making his way back to his seat too, although thanks to his fur he's a lot more slippery and slides back down. My hands feel like they're attached to the floor. I reach out to grab the wheel but slip down with a squeak, sliding into one of the windows. Luckily, no crack appears on the glass. I try again, touching the wheel with my fingertips and managing to grab on. Now I'm hanging in the air, one hand on the wheel and another dangling with my legs. I grab the wheel with my other hand and pull; it turns to the left. The whole ship clunks as it rolls upside down. A loud scratching sound echoes throughout the ship. The alarm continues to boom. Mishka rolls around on the ceiling underneath me, unable to grab onto anything.

'Yuri, turn it the right way,' Mishka shouts like I'm not already trying to do that. My hands urge to slip, I glance out the window at the aliens, they're laughing like crazy people at our struggle. My face frowns like Papa's. I look at the part of the wheel that's furthest away from me. I pull my arms up and fling out my hands, letting go of the wheel completely. I manage to grab the top and hold it tightly, the wheel spins upright with a jerk, sending the whole ship spinning around. Mishka bounces around the cabin like a ball of elastic bands, the metal booms and creaks as the ship straightens. When it evens out, I jump into my seat. We need to install seat belts to stop this from happening again.

'Mishka, man the cannons! Quickly!' I turn around to see his beady eye still spinning, it looks like he's going to need a moment to catch his *bear-ings*. Haha, I laugh to myself. The ship rumbles again, oh yeah; the aliens. Mishka tries to give me a thumbs up, but falls flat on his face. I turn forward, the aliens in the Moon Force ship are no longer laughing but watching curiously. I wave at them; their eyes go from calm to panic stations when they realise I'm about to do something unexpected.

I force the steering wheel up in the same way I had when avoiding the mountains, sending us flying towards the stars. I'm not sure if we're going up, or down, or left or right; just in a direction that pulls us away from the Moon Force. The scraping of the metal mixes with the alarms again as we zoom forward, but our speed only lasts for a few seconds. We jolt to a halt, being held back by the cable that's attached to us. Sputnik 0.5 is trying its best to pull away, but the strength of the tether is too much.

'Mishka, I need you to help me now,' I bark like the dog that lives on the street outside. Mishka's eye stops spinning as he finally balances himself on his soft feet.

'Sorry, that was some ride,' he says, the serious tone returning to his voice. Mishka runs over to his seat and pulls on a bright red lever, I can feel the fire splutter out of our engine towards the attackers, hopefully it will melt their ships. The creaking returns, filling the room with loud blaring noises that make my ears shake, the volume keeps getting louder and louder until…

The creak ends in a snap and our ship flings into space with the force of a spinning yo-yo. I can't see past the smoke that covers Sputnik 0.5's front window, so we sit and twirl, free from the Moon Force's grasp. After what feels like hours, our ship begins to steady as the smoke clears. In front of us, we can see the big wide Earth again. Even as the alarm sounds, it's still the prettiest thing I've ever seen. My mind wanders to Nastya for some reason as I look upon it, causing my chest to twinge. I'm looking at the world and all I can think of is her.

'Yuri, we're not free just yet!' Mishka's gruff voice is barely audible over the alarm. In front of us, the main alien ship flies into view, two large cannons poking out of its green surface. I can see the alien captain yell something that I can't hear, then two missiles come flying toward us.

I can't even hear myself think over the noise. The missiles collide with Sputnik 0.5, blowing us into a million pieces.

***

Mishka and I come rolling out of the spaceship onto the front carpet of the living room.

'Mayday, mayday!' I shout, causing Babushka to hurry in.

'Mechtatel! We're trying to listen to the radio, will you stop being so loud. We can hear you screaming from the kitchen,' she coughs heavily into the handkerchief she's holding. I see a splutter of red cover the fabric before she quickly hides it in her pocket.

'Sorry Babushka, Mishka and I were attacked by aliens and they blew us up. Of course I was screaming, we nearly died in space,' I can barely see her through my cardboard helmet, poking the holes through with a pencil and not making them bigger wasn't my greatest idea.

My eyes go wide again, 'and Babushka, I saw a Zilant while I was up there, over Kazan, just like you said in your stories.'

Her eyes brighten at the mention of her name.

Mama walks in behind Babushka, 'what's all this about aliens and dragons?' She looks down to the toppled over Sputnik 0.5, fixating on the tear at the top of the box; her eyes move back to me.

'That's white carpet so I hope that paint isn't still wet,' Babushka says, before smiling at Mama and leaving the room.

Mama pretends to choke herself with one of her hands, making me laugh. Mama's version of Poschekotat' Ruku, Dushit' Ruku[17], doesn't like to tickle but strangle instead. Her hand monster only comes out when Babushka isn't around. Luckily, it hasn't possessed her and chased me around yet - I'll have to improve my hiding place if it does.

'Dinner will be ready soon, we're having stewed pork and carrots,' Mama says as she exits the room. I knew I could smell it. I follow her out of the room, leaving Mishka to watch Sputnik 0.5. Tomorrow

[17] The Strangle Hand.

morning, we'll write our letter and send it to the Union's space program. They won't be able to handle the Moon Force without us - and we'll definitely beat them next time.

Sunday 29th September, 1957.

City 40, Chelyabinsk Oblast, Russian SFSR, Soviet Union.

The noise is like nothing I've ever heard before. Mishka, Vitor and I were sleeping soundly in our bedroom when it happened, waking us all up and causing our building to shake. Opening my eyes, the room is filled with a blinding light. I can't see anything, my entire body shakes with the rest of the building. My ears can't hear anything over the screeching, painful noise. I get out of bed and run over to the open window, pulling the curtains back quickly. I watch as a cloud of smoke and fire rises up into the sky, trying to touch the universe with its burning swollen finger. I can't look for longer than a few moments. My eyes feel like they're on fire, I turn away and wipe the tears that are streaming down my cheeks. I'm not crying, honest, they're just leaking. A strong wind blows through the gap in the window, causing my skin to itch on contact. I try to reach up and shut it, the closer I get the more my bones feel like they want to crawl out of my fingers.

I watch as the dust sprints away from the fiery mushroom, the top of the cloud looks as if it's almost paused in the air, gradually starting to curl over itself. It's like the launch of a rocket into space, the smoke distorting the landscape like a portal to another world.

I turn to Vitor, watching as he cowers under his blanket. A slam echoes from somewhere in the apartment. Mama's shouting and crying. Babushka flings open the door with a bang, her eyes setting on me standing next to the window with horror, her eyes glance up into the cloud. She turns away quickly and raises a hand to her face.

'Get away from the windows! Get away from the windows!' She runs over and pushes me aside, slamming the window shut after I'd failed to do so and pulling the curtains together with her wrinkly hands. I can only watch as Papa sprints past our bedroom, trying his best to pull a scary looking mask over his face.

'You all need to stay in the house, don't open the windows. I'll be back as soon as possible, I just need to find out what's happening,' he shouts into the apartment without looking at anyone in particular.

'Nizhny, we need to go back to Nizhny,' he stutters like a crazy person, his voice muffled.

The front door opens with a whoosh before slamming shut just as quickly. I can hear the steps echoing frantically from the corridor as he runs down them. Mama sprints past my doorway and flings the front door wide open again.

'Nizhny? What? Alexei? You can't go, Alexei, it's too dangerous! Alexei?'

The lobby doesn't reply, Papa has already gone. I can hear Vitor sobbing.

Our building is making so much noise; babies are crying, children are screaming, dust collects on the carpet from the shaking walls. My curtains are only thin, so the orange light still shines through intently in the darkness. I have to close my eyes - but even when they're shut the sting is like somebody has dipped them in vinegar, forcing them to open again. Mama's kneeling, sobbing in the hallway, sitting on her ankles with her head in her hands. Still facing the open doorway, she waits for Papa to change his mind and come back.

Babushka shuffles over, her cough has immediately become worse, maybe the dust that flew in after the explosion has gotten stuck in her throat. I have to close my eyes again, my face feels sunburnt, like I've spent an entire day at Lake Irtyash.

'Do you think they launched Sputnik early?' I can hear Mishka ask, but this isn't the Kazakh SSR, this is Chelyabinsk Oblast, and this isn't the time for braintalking.

The light from the window starts to dim, the vivid glow turning soft in our bedroom. A shock jolts up my spine as an arm wraps around me, my warm face nestles instinctively into rough pyjamas. It's Vitor, he holds me tightly with his eyes closed; I wonder if his sting as much as mine. My tummy churns like I've eaten poisoned pierogi[18], this is how we stay until the morning sun returns to our room.

***

My head feels strange, like I've been thrown around the room without moving. The fluid that leaks from my nose dribbles down my cheeks faster than I can wipe it away, hardening into a solid state on the side of my face. I'm not looking in a mirror, but I can feel my eyes glowing the same colour as ripe tomatoes, tingling when they're open, burning when they're closed. All I can manage to do from my bed is stare at the ceiling through my watering eyes, only moving when my belly decides to empty itself - be that through the top or the bottom.

---

[18] Filled dumplings boiled in water and often pan-fried before serving.

Vitor and Mama are taking it in turns to offer food that I say no to and forcing me to drink hot tea or cold water, their reasoning changing each time. *'Mechtatel, drink this tea you're freezing to touch'*, *'Yuri, your forehead feels like a campfire, drink this water'*, *'Now you're as cold as Siberian winter, I'll make you some tea.'*

I feel so dazed, every time I close my eyes the pain causes me to open them again, yet the room always feels like it's been moved around. Somebody is always in my room with me - yet it's never Babushka. Apparently, she's also bedridden in her own room. Mama's talking about putting us in the same place to keep each other company. Papa still hasn't come back from work. It doesn't make any sense; radios aren't important at a time like this.

I've been ill before and I don't doubt that I'll feel better again tomorrow, but I think I'll try and get off school tomorrow by faking it. I don't like the idea of seeing Dimitri, Mikhail and Nastya. Two of them are probably planning to beat me up, the other is probably planning on not talking to me. Would faking it make Alikhan more of a target? Marlen can handle himself, but I'm not so sure about the Kazakh. My stomach churns, pushing my classmates from my mind and filling my mouth with more thin saliva that stings to swallow back down.

Nobody knows anything about that big explosion last night. None of us have any idea why we have to stay away from the windows, it's only because that's what Papa said, but he gave us no explanation why. I can see out of the window from my bed, I can't see anybody outside walking around, maybe they heard Papa shout to stay indoors too. The strangest thing about everything that happened last night was Vitor hugging me. He's never been like that before, and now today he's not laughed at me or bullied me once - he's helping Mama with everything, like he's trying to distract himself.

It's only Mishka in the room with me at the moment, but I don't feel up to braintalking. The thoughts that circle my brain are as painful as my throat and eyes, so I just sit and stare at his fuzzy face and wait to fall asleep or pass out, whichever arrives first. His hazel button eye watches me intently, the lumps of sticky fur on his face clumping around his sewn-on mouth. It's as though he's staring through me and into the wall behind me, like I'm not even here.

***

I'm still in my bedroom when I come to, yet the room feels different somehow, stuffier. I keep my eyes closed as I scan the feeling of the room. My stomach has started to feel lighter - probably because I've put nothing in it for hours. It does seem ready to be filled again though. Not fighting the feeling of illness gives my ears more room to listen, a steady but heavy breathing bounces around the room. It's not nasally enough to be Vitor, but too loud and croaky with each breath to be Mama or Papa. I roll over to my other side and creak open one eye, Babushka's sleeping soundly on Vitor's bed. The sheets are hers, they must have moved her when I was asleep.

My vision crawls over to Mishka, he's still sitting in the same place as before, yet his head has fallen to the side as if he's confused at the events unfolding in front of him.

'Yuri, are you awake?' He asks through my thoughts, his stitched mouth closed.

'Just about, how long was I asleep?'

'I can't tell the time, I'm a bear, but definitely for a while. How are you feeling?'

'My body hurts all over, my eyes are still sore, but I don't feel as sick anymore,' I blink in his direction. All this braintalking isn't helping my aching body, but it's nice to talk to somebody who isn't myself.

'I'm sure you'll be fine by dinner,' Mishka chirps, 'or tomorrow morning at the latest.'

'Yeah,' I don't tell him anything else, I can surprise him by saying that I'm staying off tomorrow, but I have to get the day off from Mama first.

'When did they move Babushka in here?'

'Probably around an hour ago, it's great that she's in here don't you think?'

I raise my eyebrow confused, the slightest head movement causes the cold sweat stuck between me and my pillow to move, making the side of my face shiver. Mishka keeps up his stare, like he's waiting for a kopeck[19] to drop.

After I don't respond for a while, he speaks again.

'She can help you write your letter!'

I'm about to respond but hear movement in the hallway, a conversation between Vitor and Mama becomes audible. I try my best to focus on their conversation. Mishka becomes a wall of silence as soon as I stop listening to him.

'Do you think they'll be okay? They've done nothing but come in and out of consciousness for hours,' Vitor sounds strained, exhausted, and concerned. It's incredibly unfamiliar.

'I-I'm sure they've both just come down with something. Erm, you know, you were ill just a few weeks ago yourself Vitor. They've probably caught that, yeah that's it, definitely,' Mama's tone is shrill and high-pitched. Her voice carries a stammer that she's never had before.

'You know that's a lie, they don't look like they're getting better. There was an explosion last night, why is everyone pretending there wasn't? Papa knows what's going on, that's why he hasn't come back. He's hiding it all from us Mama, why else would he talk about going back to Nizhny immediately after the

---

[19] Soviet penny.

blast? That seems like a big call to make while he's rushing out the door.'

There's silence for a moment, all I can hear is Babushka's heavy breathing. The floorboards creak, so I close my eyes gently, not too tight so I can still see through the small gap between my eyelids. Vitor peers through the doorway, looking carefully at us both. He looks like a floating head from here as he croons around. Once satisfied, he disappears, and the conversation starts up again, his voice much calmer this time.

'It has to have been from Mayak, Mama, why else would Papa run away? Tell us to get away from the windows?'

Mama doesn't say anything.

'And if it isn't anything to do with that, then there's no reason for me not to go and check on Polina? I'm worried about her. I want to know if she's okay and nobody in their house is answering the phone,' Vitor's voice wobbles like jelly at the mention of Polina's name.

Mama still doesn't say anything.

'Fine then, I'm leaving,' I watch as Vitor storms past the doorway towards the front door. An arm grabs him softly, causing him to stop. He could easily force his way out of Mama's grasp, but it's like he wants to be told to stay. His arm still seems tense, like half of him still wants to bolt out of the door to Polina. He seems to be waiting for what Mama has to say, waiting patiently for a break in the tears that stream down her face.

'Please don't, Rybka[20],' Vitor turns to her at the sound of that foreign name, his face scrunching into one large wrinkle as he plummets into her breast, allowing his arms to wrap around her. Mama holds him tightly.

'I don't know what's happening or what to do,' she sniffles before grabbing his face and forcing him to look at her, 'but I need you to be strong for me. I can't do this alone.'

He glances into my room where Babushka and I are *sleeping*, he looks back at Mama and nods before joining her again in an embrace. It looks like Vitor has a nickname after all, I wonder where it's been hiding this whole time.

***

Not long after their conversation, Babushka begins to stir. Her rancid cough sounds like it's been mixed with gravel. I've kept my eyes sewn shut like Mishka's mouth up until now, but her loud waking up sequence gives me the perfect time to fake it. I probably shouldn't have listened to Mama and Vitor's moment together. I feel like Mikhail, the slushatel. The feeling makes me uneasy. I don't like the idea of being Mikhail in any situation, so I'm just going to

[20] Fish.

keep it to myself. Mishka heard too of course, but that's because he's always listening. If anything, he's the real slushatel in this house.

I pretend to wake up when Babushka starts coughing. Mama's already shot through the door like a bullet at the sound of noise from our newly shared room, two black teas already in hand.

'Good afternoon, you pair,' Mama says, placing the cups down on the bedside table. I look over at Babushka who's already sitting up and sipping her tea. I shuffle up and lean my pillow onto the backboard, nestling myself upright and taking my own hot tea into my hands.

Mama's folding up some laundry and putting it away into mine and Vitor's drawers with needle-point precision, Babushka sips her tea between coughs. I try to imitate her, the sipping not the coughing, but end up burning my tongue on the scorching hot beverage. Some talents must come to you as you get older.

Babushka forces a small half-smile at me, 'my parents used to call me Past' Drakona[21],' she wheezes a cough, causing her cup to shake. Maybe it's just a talent I'll never have, maybe a Zilant came to visit her when she was little and it gave her dragon powers.

Mama finishes her folding and sits down at the foot of my bed, placing her hand on the blanket, over the outline of my leg and squeezing it tightly.

---

21 Dragon Mouth.

'How are you feeling, Mechtatel?' She smiles, 'are you still feeling sick?'

I think about her question for a moment. I don't feel better yet, but I definitely feel less sick than I did earlier, probably because I haven't eaten since yesterday. I fumble with the tea in my hands, the mug is warm and feels nice on my cold fingers. I can feel the sweat across my forehead, my body feels so confused. The queasiness gets louder the more I drink, I look over to Babushka who's also waiting for me to answer.

'I don't really know,' I say. Mama's face drops, her grasp on my leg squeezes harder almost instinctively, she turns to Babushka.

'And you feel the same?'

'Something doesn't feel right my dear, but I guess everyone thinks that when they're ill,' she smiles encouragingly at Mama, who seems much happier with her response than mine.

'Vitor is helping me cook dinner today, what do you fancy? We were thinking pelmeni? I know it's one of your favourites, Mechtatel.'

Babushka's stomach growls angrily, putting Mishka to shame with its volume, his roar is always more of a whimper. Although silent, mine too turns upside down at the thought. I never thought I'd ever feel sick at the mention of pelmeni.

'Hey, I hope that's not because I'm cooking,' Vitor barks from the other room, jokingly offended.

His response to Babushka's gurgling belly draws a smile from everyone in the room, even me.

'Not at all dear,' Babushka splutters, 'it's just that…'

'I think it'll help,' Mama smiles forcefully, interrupting her and not taking no for an answer. She walks out the room, insisting that we need food under her breath while she heads to help Vitor knead the dough for the dumplings. Babushka and I try to protest, but she's already left the room. Seems to me like we're only eating to make her feel better, or to give her and Vitor something to do while everyone's stuck inside.

The room falls silent, leaving me with the sound of Babushka's heavy breathing. She sips on her tea with a slurp, before smacking her lips together and placing it back on her lap. Mishka's staring at me, I know what he's thinking - that while I'm bedridden I might as well write my letter. My pencils and paper are on the side table, just waiting for me to ask for them.

'Babushka, can you pass me my writing stuff please?'

She glances over her shoulder and places her tea on the bedside table with a wobble, who knew placing down hot drinks would be so difficult when you're old? Grabbing everything I asked for, she passes them over to me, holding them out in my direction with the same wobble. I balance my tea dangerously on my lap and reach over with my tongue spilling out, causing Babushka to scowl.

'Mechtatel, you're going to burn yourself if you're not careful.'

'I'll be fine,' I say, grabbing them, knocking my cup slightly but steadying it with my free hand. Babushka's eyes widen, only settling after she's sure of my safety.

'Vitor said the same thing when he was your age, right before knocking his own tea into his lap. He needed an ice bath after that, his thighs were bright red and scolded, and you should have seen his little…'

'Babushka! Please! Stop it,' Vitor pleads from the kitchen, 'he really doesn't need to hear that, and I don't need reminding.'

I can hear Mama sniggering from the other room.

Babushka giggles quietly too, I can't help but laugh back because her laugh is so infectious. It causes the pain in my throat to jab me abruptly, ceasing my good time. The sickness in my stomach gurgles at me, wiping the smile straight off my face as fast as it had appeared. I clutch it without thinking and wait for it to pass, the last thing I want is to run off to the bathroom again. There's nothing left to get rid of, so why is my stomach still begging to be emptied?

'What are you drawing?' She asks, obviously trying to take my mind off my belly. A gasp escapes my lips. I can feel a burn at the back of my throat, like lava's trying to crawl its way out of my mouth but it's stuck tickling the bottom of the dangly thing I can see when I brush my teeth.

'I'm not drawing anything,' I cough with a snort like Babushka normally does, causing the molten rock to sizzle in my throat, 'I'm writing a letter.'

I take the pencil in my hand and place it on the top right of the paper, just as I go to start scribbling, Babushka speaks again.

'A letter? And who is that going to? The girl from the party? I noticed you couldn't stop looking at her, my little Casanova'

I know that she always watches me, but I'd barely looked in Nastya's direction yesterday. How could she have spotted me? Not like she would have spotted anything though, because there was nothing to spot in the first place. I can see Mishka staring at me from the corner of my eye, as though he actually believes Babushka as well. The betrayal.

'No. She's nobody, and she's Polina's sister so that would be weird,' I say sternly, mainly so Babushka would stop talking. My pencil touches the paper again, eager to start its journey. Babushka chuckles and starts up again, seemingly intent on stopping me from writing.

‘I wouldn’t say it’s weird at all, it’s happened a lot throughout history,’ she scratches the curly hairs on her chin, thinking of examples.

‘Babushka,’ I protest, ‘I don’t like girls and she’s Vitor’s girlfriend’s sister and we’re not even getting on at the moment. She won’t talk to me at all,’ my face burns red, despite me trying my best to hide it.

‘Okay, Mechtatel, you can think what you want,’ she slurps on her tea heavily, finishing the cup and placing it down gently in her lap. Now that’s over with, I steady my pencil on the page again, *finally* starting my letter.

‘Have you got a girlfriend you’re not telling me about?’ Mishka asks, under that face he’s frowning, I can tell.

‘Who’s the letter for then?’ Babushka decides that she’s back in the conversation. I’m never going to get started at this rate.

‘I'm writing to the government to tell them about my trip to space, and my battle with the Moon Force and my plans for the Sputnik 1 launch because I’ve been to space before anyone else. If I don’t write it and send it soon then I'm not going to get to go,’ I raise my voice a bit too loudly at the end. Babushka stares at me like I’ve got four heads.

‘A letter to Khrushchev? That’s very exciting, maybe you could say hello to him from your old Babushka?’

I roll my eyes, she catches them and huffs loudly.

'Fine, what about all those days and nights where I bathed you and looked after you while your mama and papa were busy. But it's fine, my own grandchild won't even write me a hello to the Chairman, even if he's not as great as Joe…' she tails off to herself.

'Okay, fine, I'll tell him you said hello,' I just want her to stop talking.

'You should have said yes the first time,' Mishka butts in.

'Sorry Babushka.'

'Well maybe you can invite your girlfriend to come with you,' she chuckles. Just as I'm about to answer, she pierces the air with a screech, causing my eardrums to shatter like broken glass.

'Mila! Can I get another cup of tea?'

'Okay Duscha, give me a second, we're just finishing the pelmeni dough.'

I look over to Babushka who's reaching over to grab her empty mug from the bedside, her frail arms wobbling more intensely.

***

Dear First Secretary Khrushchev,

I'm writing to tell you about my first visit to space. Me and my bear, Mishka, launched from City 40 in Chelyabinsk Oblast from my mama and papa's apartment, over the Urals and into space in our rocket Sputnik 0.5.

After a successful launch, we were found by the Moon Force and they shot us back down to Earth. Our experience in space means that we are perfect to be launched with Sputnik 1, as part of the crew that tackles the Moon Force. Needs must as this is a matter of experience.

No training is needed as we have already had one successful launch, but something to stop the giant claw on the bottom of their spaceship would be incredibly helpful.

Thank you,

Yuri Rubinov.

P.S. My Babushka says hello, she made me add this to the letter.

I fold the piece of paper into a square, I can't have this being read by the wrong people, far too many already know about the Sputnik 1 project. I place it on top of my blanket. I'm sure Mama has envelopes tucked away in a drawer somewhere.

'Mama?' I shout weakly into the hallway, 'do you have any envelopes? Please may I have one?'

'Yes Mechtatel, I'll get Vitor to bring one in for you.'

‘Thank you, Mama,’ I squeak like a field mouse, my voice too strained from shouting. I catch Babushka’s smile in my direction, although I’m not too sure what it’s for.

I sit and play with my fingers while I wait, Vitor will probably come in, throw the envelope in my face, punch me in the arm and push me out of bed. Then he’ll probably…

‘Here you go,’ he enters the room and places it at my side gently, ‘dinner will be ready soon, I think we’re eating it in here with you both,’ he smiles a little and walks out. Who is this and what have they done with my brother?

I grab my pencil and write the address that Mrs. Palakova had given me on the front of the envelope, I’ve read it so many times that I can recall it from memory:

First Secretary Khrushchev
Tsentrosoyuz Building
Moscow
Soviet Union, 101000

I place my letter onto the bedside counter closest to me. I'll ask Mama to post it tomorrow when everything is back to normal and I'm pretending to be sick to get off school. I watch Vitor walk past the doorway towards the telephone. Papa says we’re very lucky to have a telephone in our apartment and that the rest of the Union can only dream of having one. Vitor's been trying to call Polina's house all day but nobody's picking up. Do they even have a phone? Maybe he's just been dialling random numbers. After a moment he shuffles past the doorway again, this time in the other direction, head down, defeated, she mustn't have picked up again. I hope Nastya's okay too.

Not long afterwards, Mama and Vitor bring through the vegetable pelmeni they've spent all this time preparing. I try to eat some, I really do, but whether it's Vitor's cooking or that fact I already feel ill, my belly immediately rejects it and I have to run to the bathroom. Babushka manages to keep one down, but never reaches for another, instead keeping her eyes closed, trying her best to keep it there.

Papa still hasn't come home. I hope that he's doing okay. My stomach growls at me like it's filled with sewage. I watch myself in the bathroom mirror, my eyes sting as they blink. I might not have to pretend to get off school tomorrow.

Monday 30th September, 1957.

City 40, Chelyabinsk Oblast, Russian SFSR, Soviet Union.

Mama wakes me up screaming, jolting my eyes open like I've been shocked with electricity. My face is wet, and the smell is horrifying, apparently, I'd thrown up on my pillow in the night and slept right through it. It's only sick, why is she so scared? The curdling nature of her strained voice is like she's seen a dead body. She drags me straight to the bathroom and helps me clean myself off. I still don't feel right at all - my head feels so foggy that I can barely see anything, even though my vision is completely fine.

I don't even have to try and talk myself into staying off school, Mama tells me that she won't be letting me, or Vitor go until Papa comes back and gives us the all clear. One of the craziest things about this explosion is the discovery that radios might be the most important thing in the Union, to the point where Papa has to check they're okay before he checks on us. I think of the radio in our front room. Should I go and make sure it's okay? I wonder if Sanzhar had rushed off as well, wouldn't that mean Alikhan is on his own? What if he's sick too? And anyway, why do workers in a radio factory know so much about secret government satellites?

Thinking about Alikhan makes me worry about Nastya, which makes me feel a bit guilty, but it's only her that my foggy brain wants to think of. I hope Polina calls today and tells Vitor that everything is fine, that Nastya is fine. It's funny how I worry about her more than everybody else, despite our argument the other day. Vitor isn't happy about being told he can't go to school, he had thrown his bag into Mama and stormed off into Babushka's old room, locking the door behind him. Mama's face was wet when she came into our room with tea afterwards, but I didn't want to say anything. Vitor makes me cry too.

'Still no sign of Alexei?' Babushka asks, ignoring the earlier incident with Vitor.

'Nothing, not even a call from the facility,' Mama is blunt, her hand shakes like Babushka's when she'd raised her tea to her mouth yesterday.

'I'm sure he'll be home soon; he's probably just investigating what happened. It's most likely a huge coincidence,' I notice Babushka and Mama looking at me for some reason, I wish they'd leave me out of these boring grown-up conversations.

'Mama,' I butt in, grabbing the letter from the side, 'can you post this today? I need it to arrive as soon as possible,' I hand her my envelope. She studies the address on the front like I'd openly asked her to read it.

'Ah, so this is the letter I've heard all about,' she flips it over, even though there isn't anything written on the other side.

'Did you say hello from me?' Babushka asks.

'Yes, Babushka, I did.'

'Excellent,' she shoots me a weak wink before laying her head down back on the cushion with a huff, 'I feel exhausted Mila, instead of tea can we have coffee next time? I think it may help.'

'I'm just worried it will upset your stomach,' Mama replies.

'My stomach is already weeping, what more could possibly happen to it?'

Then the telephone starts to ring. Vitor thunders out of the room he had locked himself in and runs straight to the device, picking it up immediately.

'Hello, Rubinov residence, Vitor speaking.'

Babushka, Mama, Mishka and I are silent as we try our hardest to listen to his conversation.

'I'm glad to hear from you--'

'--yes, but at least--'

'I understand, Yuri and Babushka are the same here--'

'--and Nastya?'

My heart feels like it's standing at the edge of Mount Narodnaya.

'Oh, she's fine? That's a relief--'

The sinking feeling evaporates from my body, replaced by the overwhelming urge to see her.

'It must have been something to do with that explosion--'

'--did you watch it from the window?'

'I knew it-- wait, right now?'

'I love you…'

His voice tails off, the words he'd said hang in the air like drying laundry. I've never heard him say the 'L' word to any of us at home, so to hear him say it to Polina is shocking. We all wait in awkward silence for him to come into the room, on edge for what feels like twenty minutes. Finally, the plastic clink of the phone back into its receiver echoes around the apartment.

'Vitor?' Mama asks.

'She's the same, vomiting, not eating…'

Mama's head turns to me and Babushka, forcing a smile, before standing and leaving the room in a hurry, making sure to close the door behind her, the letter still lingering on my bedside.

***

Mama and Vitor have been gone for a while, Babushka had finished her tea and fell asleep too. The coffee would have probably kept her awake for a bit longer, but after listening to Vitor's telephone conversation it had never arrived.

So now I'm left with Mishka. Even though I'm tired and not feeling great, he's always in the mood to talk - and besides, it might just help me fall asleep hearing his voice. Plus, it would be good to talk about the mission, as a bit of a pick-me-up, everyone else seems so sad at the moment.

'I can't believe she left the letter in here; doesn't she know the Moon Force is still out there? It'll only take so long until they come down to Earth and destroy it. They could have been behind that explosion for all we know. We need to be at that launch,' he says, his head still hunching like it had been yesterday.

'I'm sure she will, she's just waiting for Papa to come home. I should have asked Mrs. Palakova for a phone number, it would have been so much faster,' I braintalk back to him, my eyes fluttering with the idea of sleep, my pillow has never felt so comfortable.

'I don't think they give out the government's number easily, especially one where you can talk directly to Khrushchev. I'm actually surprised that you managed to get an address.'

'Maybe Mrs. Palakova is a spy.'

Mishka stares blankly and laughs into my brain, 'teachers would make the worst spies, I don't think you'd be able to get much information from children. Especially from your school, unless they want to know how many kozyavki[22] Marlen eats a day.'

'You never know, kids are smart too,' I justify myself to him, and to be fair, the number that he eats is quite impressive, if not massively disgusting.

'Yeah, sure, whatever.'

I pretend that his comment doesn't hurt my feelings, after all, I'm the one going to space, not Babushka or Papa or Mama or Sanzhar or Mrs. Palakova or Mr. Dragunov. It's me, Yuri Rubinov, a child. Mishka too, but not if he carries on down this train of thought.

He seems to sense that I didn't like what he said, crawling off the chest he had been sitting on and walking over to my bedside. He rubs his mouth with his furry paw, seemingly dislodging the sewing around his mouth, allowing it to move freely like everybody else's. Mishka breathes in heavily, taking in the air of my bedroom.

'I wonder what the Moon Force is up to now, surely there's something special that they're hiding up there,' he looks towards the ceiling of the room, but I

---

[22] Bogeys.

think he means even higher than that. I really doubt there's anything interesting on the floor above ours.

'Maybe the Moon really is made of cheese, or maybe it's the mitochondria of the solar system, like it's all one big cell keeping us all alive,' I say.

'I'm pretty sure that's the Sun,' Mishka says sarcastically. I don't even bother to respond to his joke, I'm not in the mood.

'Or maybe it's just a big rock where they live,' Mishka chuckles, 'or maybe they're just protective about the view.'

'You're probably right, it's always the silly guesses that end up being the correct ones,' I watch him strut around the room in peacock-like fashion.

I feel like my head is underwater as I watch him, like it's bobbing around the surface of a lake, my vision going blurry whenever the water washes over me. I can't concentrate on the stuffed bear strutting around my room. He turns and walks towards Babushka, looking up at her with his one beady eye; it follows her chest as she breathes in and out with a slight wheeze.

'I can see where Vitor gets his heavy breathing from, luckily you don't have it yet, I wouldn't be able to sleep a wink if I had to sleep with my ear next to that. Has her snoring been keeping you awake too?'

All I can do is listen, my body is exhausted, my vision gradually going blurry. My chest grows tighter and full of gunk. Mishka's vision falls to me, his normally smiling mouth turning to a Papa-style frown, the eyebrows that normally hang proudly on his face droop.

'Listen, I know that your Mama said she'd deliver it later, but I don't think it's going to arrive fast enough. I'm going to go and post it now, just to make sure,' he grabs the letter from my bed with the hairy fingers that seemed to grow out of his stubby paw, before swinging the door open and walking out.

That's so nice of him, I think to myself as I slowly drift off to sleep.

***

The letter is missing when I wake up. I look over to the side of the room where Mishka had previously been sitting on the chest, where his tilted head hadn't moved in days. He isn't there either. He's nestled in the gap between my arm and my body, cosying up to me because I don't snore loudly like the rest of my family.

'How did that bear of yours end up there?' Babushka asks.

I just stare at his scruffy one-eyed face. I honestly have no idea. I reach out to braintalk to him, but he's not responding. Did he really deliver my letter?

A weak ray of sunshine bounces into my eyes, distracting me from Mishka. There's no clock in the room for me and Babushka to tell the time, her or

Mama are my normal alarm clocks. The sky is setting into a sunset, causing orange to spill into the room like it had last night. My entire body burns at the memory.

'Mama,' I call, 'please can you shut the curtains?'

There's no response. Babushka and I are stuck in our beds with sickness. The longer the orange remains, the more I feel like my mind is going to drip out of my ears like chunky swamp water. I look down to Mishka in my arms.

'Can you get up again and do it?'

His mouth is sewn in place, his beady eye staring into space. No braintalk comes from him, just complete, deafening silence.

'Guess we'll just have to wait for the sun to go down, your butler seems to be taking a nap,' Babushka chuckles with her regular rasp.

***

About two hours later the hunger returns. The sickness instantly rises from my body, leaving behind a starvation I've never felt before. Babushka feels the same, we crawl out of the bedroom like animals and dart straight to the kitchen, where Mama and Vitor are sitting with soaked faces and their heads in their hands. Whatever they've been talking about, they quickly brush it under the carpet and pretend it isn't there.

'Ah, good evening,' Mama wipes the underside of her eyes with the back of her wrist, leaving black smudges where her makeup was. Vitor sits in silence.

'We feel much better,' I say. Vitor's eyes dart from me to the phone, rolling out the hunch in his shoulders, making himself sit upright.

'Really?' Mama inhales a breath sharply, a tear rolls down her cheek, 'I'm so happy to hear that.'

She pulls Babushka into a tight but tender hug, Babushka's shoulder growing moist from her face. She suddenly pulls away and kneels to my height, placing her hands either side of my face and squeezing my cheeks.

'You must be so hungry; I'll make whatever you want. If we have it in the cupboards of course.'

I think for a moment, I don't want anything too spicy or pickled. I look up at Mama.

'Blini[23]?'

Just thinking about it, I can already taste the pancakes with a thick spread of homemade jam. Ooh I wonder if Mama has any honey?

'Are you happy with that Duscha?' She glances at Babushka, who simply shrugs.

'I could eat a scabby dog, dear,' she smiles.

'Great, great. I'm sure Vitor's fine with that too, they were his favourite as a boy,' my brother just shrugs his shoulders, his face absent of colour but slowly regaining its shade.

---

23 Russian pancakes.

It's then we hear a noise, a light tapping fills the room, like fingernails on a tabletop. We all look at each other, then to the table, only Vitor's hands are there, but they're flat and stretched out. His fingernails are too stubby from years of chewing them to even make a tapping sound. It would be a fleshy thud even if it was him. It's then that Babushka hisses between her teeth, stumbling towards the windowsill where a crow has perched itself - its beak tapping on the window. She punches the pane lightly, not hard enough to smash, but loud enough to make a bang and scare the bird away. Turning back around, her face pale, Vitor's head is in his hands again. Even Mama doesn't know where to look.

It's said that a tapping bird on your window is a terrible omen.

***

We're just finishing off our blini when the door opens, the turn of the key makes me jump out of my seat, sprinting over to the door and waiting for whoever's outside to open it. Not that there's a shadow of a doubt who it is. Everybody else follows behind. I'm feeling much better, I can't wait to tell Papa that everything is okay, that Babushka and I are hungry again, and that my eyes don't sting as much.

The door squeaks open as Papa limps in, his legs needing him to think about what he's doing, otherwise he'll fall over. He's pale, the white of his uniform is dirty and tattered, making him look similar to a muddy ghost. The black around his eyes makes the red veins inside them pop out, like his eyes have also been dipped in vinegar. He's holding his hat in his hands. Although Papa is looking right at us, it feels like he's looking straight through. He coughs heavily into his hands, dropping his hat accidentally.

I scramble to pick it up like I always do and run as fast as I can into the kitchen.

'Poschekotat' Ruku! You'll never be able to catch me,' I hide under the kitchen table and wait for the hand to find me, to tickle me until I feel like I'm going to cry from laughter. But it never comes, no taunting, no footsteps, nothing. I poke my head out from under the table, Papa's not even moved from the doorway.

'Alexei, is it safe to go outside?' Mama asks.

Papa's vision turns from me to her, 'the higher ups say it is, but I don't believe them.'

Everyone stays quiet.

'They're all talking about being selected for scientific purposes, that it's vital we stay. Fuck that,' Papa never curses, yet the words roll off his tongue like snake venom, 'we're leaving in the morning, back to Nizhny. It's not safe here.'

'Should we start packing?' Babushka says.

'What about Polina?' Vitor interjects.

'We can't just up and move in one night!' Mama panics.

All I can think about is Nastya.

'Enough!' Papa yells, I've never heard him raise his voice like that before, he's always been so softly spoken, even when he's angry. His eyeballs bounce around his sockets like they can't focus in one particular place.

'I am exhausted. All I know is we're leaving, no ifs or buts. Did everyone stay away from the windows?'

A silence falls across the room, his eyes shoot between us all like dragonflies across a lake.

'Babushka and Yuri, they were close to the windows. They've been ill, but they're feeling much better now. We had some blini for dinner, would you like some?' Mama's words seemingly fall on deaf ears.

His eyes move agonisingly down to me under the table, it's a look that I've never seen before. He doesn't pull his usual frown, his lips wobble, he raises his hands to his mouth to cough again but the sound is different, forced even. When he moves his hands away his face is wet.

Papa staggers into the flat and closes the door behind him, locking it tightly. He places a hand on Babushka's arm and squeezes lovingly, his eyes trying their best to smile at her, before walking through to the kitchen in silence and grabbing a bottle of vodka straight from the cupboard.

He turns back and kneels down to me, opening his hand out for his hat. I place it there gently as he forces a smile.

'Thank you, Mechtatel, I'm not in the mood to play today. We will when we're back in Nizhny,' he ruffles my hair. When he stands, his grasp on his hat is as tight as Gertruda clutching the rucksack she'd never wanted.

Whoever this man is, he doesn't feel like my Papa. Sure, he looks like him, but something behind his eyes is different. That bottle has been there for years, he's always said he's been saving it for a special occasion. This doesn't seem very special at all. Papa walks back towards the rest of my family and waits at his bedroom door.

'It's important that we leave in the morning,' he says, before bringing the bottle to his lips and taking a large mouthful - its alien taste causing him to wince slightly.

He enters and slams the door behind him, causing it to echo throughout our apartment, leaving everybody in a shocked silence. After a while, Vitor dives towards the phone and mashes in what I can only guess is Polina's home number.

***

The night is so cold that I swear I can feel the frost forming on my lips. Part of me worries that the snot that dribbles down my face will harden into ice. As my body finally starts to adjust to the frozen temperature, Babushka's heavy snoring takes its turn to keep me awake. I roll myself into my own blanket cocoon, making sure to cover my face and tuck in my feet. Mishka is cuddled into my chest, his one eye the coldest thing that rests on my skin.

'Thank you for mailing the letter,' I braintalk to him, 'I wonder when we'll hear back.'

'Hopefully soon,' he says, 'but if your Papa makes us move back to Nizhny then they won't know where we are.'

I shiver slightly, yet the sweat on my head rolls down my face like it's been boiled on the stove. Feeling better didn't last for very long, maybe a few hours at most, but now I feel worse than I did before. I think my body dropped its guard, like soldiers at war, convinced the enemy had retreated, only for them to march back to the gates when the defenders weren't looking.

I sigh, my body can't seem to decide what temperature it wants to be, whether it should feel hot or cold. What doesn't help is the stinging pain behind my eyes, chewing away at the front of my brain like a starving insect had crawled up my nose when I wasn't looking. I decide to pop my head up and look around the room. Everything has been packed away - things that didn't fit in the car will be left here until Papa thinks it's safe enough to come back. I wonder if anyone else is leaving, will I ever see Marlen, Alikhan or Nastya ever again? At least I won't have to deal with Dimitri and Mikhail. The thought of leaving when Nastya is so unhappy with me doesn't sit right, and only makes it more difficult to fall asleep; thinking of her makes me feel ill in a different way. Vitor is insisting on seeing Polina before we leave, so I'm sure I'll be able to see Nastya too before we go for good. I have to, just like he has to see Polina. I don't think I'd be able to cope otherwise.

I can't remember our life in Nizhny very well, it's where Mama, Babushka, Vitor, Mishka, and I lived before Papa was allowed to bring us here to City 40. According to them, we'd all been born there, including me. Well, except for Babushka, her roots are in Kazan with the Zilants. Papa has worked in City 40 for years, but Mama says we weren't allowed to follow him at first because of how secret it was. We were only able to come ourselves about four years ago. I was so small when we were in Nizhny, I don't remember any of my friends, or anything about our life there at all really. I wonder whether they'll remember me when we go back? Does that mean that my friends here will forget me like I've forgotten my old ones? That thought joins the mix of other things that are keeping me awake tonight.

Papa says that things will be different there - he says that we've all gotten used to nice food and telephones and presents on our birthdays, but apparently there's less of all of that there, especially food. Maybe that would be great for Vitor, but not for me, I feel like if I'm any thinner you'll be able to see through me like a window.

Apparently, things are going to be hard for a while, all of us might even have to share a bedroom, but he says it'll be worth it because we'll all be together. I know that we're taking the radio, but I hope it doesn't make Papa miss his old job too much. I wonder what he'll do next, maybe a Sputnik 2 project will be in Nizhny. I'm sure Sanzhar would put in a good word for him. On second thought, after Gertruda's birthday party, probably not. Sorry Papa.

The cold draft on my face is nice compared to being tucked under the duvet, my head feels a lot warmer than everywhere else on my body, despite feeling frozen only a couple of minutes ago.

'Do you remember anybody from Nizhny?' I ask Mishka, checking if he can't sleep either.

'No, not really. We didn't really talk much back then.'

He's right, back in Nizhny we hadn't figured out our way of talking to each other. It was only after we moved here, when Vitor got older and I didn't know anybody at school that Mishka had started talking to me, like an angel saving me from my loneliness.

'It's strange that you can feel like an alien in one place, then when it's time to leave, you don't want to, because you've become one of the aliens after all that time,' I say to him.

'Like the Moon Force,' Mishka says back.

'Yeah, like the Moon Force,' my body feels exhausted and tired. I fall asleep, even though Babushka's snoring tries its hardest to keep me awake.

Tuesday 1st October, 1957.

City 40, Chelyabinsk Oblast, Russian SFSR, Soviet Union.

The morning starts in the worst way I could have ever imagined, well, other than the explosion the other night. I'm jolted awake by a loud crash in the room, like an earthquake is happening in the bed next to mine. When my eyes open, my body feels like Vitor has sat on me in the middle of the night and my bones have been crushed. Seconds after opening them, my eyes return to feeling like they're covered in salt. I turn my head towards Babushka, her arms and legs dance as she lays there - her eyes are closed, her mouth leaping up and down like a demon is trying to escape her body and fly out of the door.

I can't do anything but sit and watch, my arms are too sore, my stomach too queasy. I just watch her dance her alien dance, like a member of the Moon Force. Her body and her bed move in tandem, like they've practised this routine so many times before.

The door flings open, crashing into the wall, adding even more noise to the room. Papa rushes in, takes one look at Babushka and tries his best to pin her down.

'Vitor! Mila! Get in here. Somebody take Yuri away,' his voice is high-pitched and strained. No words leave my mouth, I can't pull my eyes away. Mama runs in and picks me up to pull me out of the room, we barely make it through the door before I throw up all over the carpet in the hallway. The motion of being in the air is too much for my stomach to handle. My head sways from side to side as I glance back into my room, catching a glimpse of Papa and Vitor trying their hardest to stop Babushka's crazy dancing.

***

'Dance, dance, dance,' Babushka shouts, shaking her body rhythmically in the centre of the room to a distant melody. She cradles something small and furry in her hands.

I rub my eyes, they're so blurry that I can't focus on what she's holding. She launches the object into the air with a spin, and like a ballerina, the fluffy item flings its arms towards the sky and points out its leg. It's Mishka.

'Are you coming, Yuri?' He asks, sliding towards me on his knees after landing. The room we're in is pitch-black everywhere I look and I can't see anything in any direction, no matter how hard I squint. Despite the darkness, the dance floor in the centre of the room is well lit from a light that I can't quite make out, no matter which angle I try and inspect it. Babushka isn't even looking at me, she's on a planet far away with the song that plays, her body moving with the tune like the gentle sway of the ocean.

I take a moment to listen to the music she's dancing to, I have to focus my ears into the darkness to hear it. It's *'There Are So Many Golden Lights',* the one with the lyrics Babushka despises, which must be why she's humming the tune instead of singing it. She's still facing in the other direction, moving her limbs like I've never seen her do before. Babushka has always been so stiff when she walks, stiff when bringing tea to her lips, stiff when using a knife and fork - but here she's somebody else, a person who has lost all that age she carries around.

'Yuri, don't you want to join in?' Mishka tugs at my hand with his furry fingers, his paws are strangely clammy, leaving my hand feeling sticky and moist. I look over at Babushka's dancing again. I lift a foot to take a step forward, but slowly retreat it, a feeling of dread coats me like tar.

Mishka frowns. He's about to say something, but I beat him to it.

'Babushka!' I shout, she turns around to me, stopping her dancing abruptly.

'Oh, Mechtatel, are you ready to dance with me yet?' Her arms and legs still move to the rhythm of the slow accordion that snakes throughout the song.

I can't bring myself to say anything more, I look down at Mishka who's still pulling impatiently at my arm. I can hear footsteps approaching me, Babushka is walking with her old shaky movements off the wooden dance floor. She pulls me into an embrace, looking into my eyes, her hands holding my cheeks, smiling at me softly. She opens her lips to speak.

'WAKE UP!' She screams in my face, causing my ears to pop.

My eyes burst open, I'm on the floor, my hand laying in a pool of my own vomit. Mama has my face in her hands, just like Babushka had a few seconds ago.

'Thank God, you're okay,' she pulls me close, paying no mind to the smelly liquid that covers me from head to toe. My eyes glance into the bedroom again, the bed is no longer shaking, Babushka had finally stopped her dancing.

***

I'm tucked back into my bed now; a fresh pair of sheets have replaced the ones that ended up covered in vomit. I hate it when my sheets get changed, all my nose can smell is chemicals, making me feel worse when I accidentally focus on it for too long. I roll my head to look at Babushka, she's sleeping soundly, her bed no longer shaking from her dancing. Mishka is back on his perch at the other side of the room, intently watching us both do nothing.

Papa had tried to move Babushka from her bed after her performance, he said they're called tremors, but her body had collapsed to the floor and started up again. After getting her back into bed, he'd sworn loudly about Nizhny, running back to his vodka for the second time in as many days, while cursing that we'd never make it out of here. I'm surprised there's still any vodka left. Maybe there were more bottles in the same place that the first one was hiding.

Our room is still, much different than it was this morning. I listen to the conversation between Papa, Mama, and Vitor in the kitchen. They're talking like I'm not listening, but I am, so the joke's on them.

'But they were so chipper yesterday, Alexei, I don't understand why they've turned again so quickly,' the voice is Mama's, her words fall out of her mouth and grasp around for answers like searching hands. Even from here I can hear the panic in her voice.

‘I don’t know, I just know we need to get to Nizhny as soon as possible, or at least leave town,’ Papa says, ‘they can’t stay here, what if they get worse?’

‘What about Polina?’ Vitor butts in, like he has been a lot recently.

‘What about her, son? I’m trying to look out for my own family, I can’t help anybody else’s,’ he snaps back. I can only imagine the look on my brother's face.

‘When they’re feeling better again, we’ll go?’ Mama says, replying to Papa, I think.

‘That’s the plan,’ I can hear Papa swigging his vodka, ‘until then we’ll just have to wait.’

I hear a thud against the wall and a loud celebration coming from outside. It sounds like other children playing games, their shouts crawl up through my window and fill the room. I look towards Babushka, her breath is still steady - I doubt she’ll be waking up any time soon.

‘Papa, there are people playing outside, can I at least go and see Polina before we leave? I’m sure Nastya would want to see Yuri as well,’ they must have heard the shouting too. I can still hear Papa swilling his drink around his mouth, before gulping loudly.

‘Vitor, stop acting like a pochemuchka[24], you’re getting too old for this… ’

---

24 A small child who’s insatiably inquisitive.

'Alexei,' Mama snaps, 'we're leaving as soon as we can, you're uprooting us again for whatever reason and not being clear about it. Not to mention all of this drinking. We can all hear your sushnyak[25]. This is Vitor's girlfriend. They might never see each other again. Stop being completely unreasonable, we set up here because of you, you can't just expect us to drop everything and leave without saying goodbye."

There's a long pause, before I can hear the bottle scrape against the wall.

'Fine, whatever,' Papa walks out and closes the door to their bedroom. Not long after, Vitor sprints past my doorway and into the hall. All I can hear after a moment is the echoing of steps as he runs down them at full speed towards Polina.

All I can think about is Nastya. I wonder if she even wants to see me. I raise a hand to my face, it's almost like my skin is tightening around it, making it feel flaky and dehydrated. Do I even want to see her? At least my sheets are clean, but I don't want to vomit again, especially around her. That would be so embarrassing.

I look up to see Mama, who's appearing in the doorway, forcing a smile as if it's her job. She comes over and hugs me like she'll never be able to again. She squeezes me so tightly it feels like I'm going to pop.

'Do you need anything, Mechtatel?'

---

25 A dry throat from drinking.

'Water please, Mama,' maybe that will help my face feel better.

'Coming right up,' she says, standing up and heading out to grab some. Mama isn't gone for long, but when she walks back in, the words fall out of my mouth uncontrollably.

'Mama, are girls allowed to go to space?'

She thinks for a moment, placing the glass on the table next to my bed, before opening her mouth, only to close it, then open it again.

'I don't see why you'd think girls *couldn't* go to space?' She answers my question with her own, now it's my turn to scratch my head.

'But you always cooked dinner while me and Papa worked on Sputnik 0.5, you were never interested in playing, it was always Papa and my friends. And when you did, you only put one letter on?'

There's a moment of silence, suddenly broken when Mama bursts into laughter, causing Babushka to stir slightly.

'That's because if I ever played with you, or Vitor, or your Papa, we'd never be able to eat! Your father doesn't know the difference between a pot and a pan, he's useless,' she wipes a tear from her eye.

'So, I was right to tell Nastya she wasn't allowed to fly on my spaceship then, I knew it,' I nod proudly to myself and glance back up at Mama, her smile has vanished.

'You did not say that to that poor girl?'

I suddenly feel very embarrassed.

'Well, I- y-you know, erm w-ell,' my mouth lets me down.

'Yuri Alexei Rubinov, I did not raise you that way. That girl can be whatever she wants to be.'

'No, she can't, she's a girl,' Mama looks at me with eyes like hot water, but it wasn't my lips that moved, those words weren't mine. I shuffle in my bed to see Babushka wide awake.

'Duscha, he is *my* son,' Mama glares at her.

'He's *my* grandson. Talk to him like that and you'll make him soft, like a little girl. Look at Vitor, pining over this young lady he's with, you've made them both so squishy, not like real men,' Babushka snaps at the air, before looking down at me in the opposite bed and smiling. I don't think she means it personally, well, I hope she doesn't. I'm not soft, am I? I look towards Mishka for a pick-me-up, yet no comments come from his fluffy brain, he always seems to abandon me when I'm in a tight spot.

'My children are not soft, they're considerate and they're not going to act like they're superior to other people. On Earth, men and women take the same risks. Why shouldn't we be taking the same risks in space?'

It's Babushka's turn to scoff, 'but that's how the world works dear, you think I'd have been a housewife if the world had let me be an engineer? Or a politician? Or a poet? It's how the world will always be. Your ability to speak doesn't mean you're intelligent,' she spits before hunching forward into a cough that sounds like her insides are going to fall out. Mama takes the water from my bedside table with a smile and passes it over to Babushka, her eyes wet and red from coughing.

Mama rubs Babushka's back gently as she sips, they were just arguing but Mama had dropped it as soon as she saw she was struggling. It dawns on me, like I've just opened the curtains to let the sunshine in, I don't need to completely agree with someone to be friends with them. I look over to Mishka again, I sure don't agree with everything that he comes out with. The same can be said for Marlen or Alikhan or most of my family, but I'm still friends with all of them. I still love them.

'Duscha, the world will change someday, Stalin was a heartless man who let his son Yakov die in a German concentration camp, but he too adored his first wife and treated her with dignity. If a man like that can treat his wife well, so can my sons,' she stops stroking her back and leaves the room for something, Babushka still sips on my water, her throat probably too sore for talking.

When the silence comes back to the room, my queasiness returns with it, but whether that's because of my illness, or for Nastya, I still can't tell the difference.

***

The door opens again at about three in the afternoon, or at least it *feels* like three in the afternoon, judging by the position of the sun outside. Vitor has brought Nastya back with him, but Polina is nowhere to be seen, apparently too bedridden to even attempt the walk. I think back to this morning, the vomit on my face, Babushka trying her hardest to get me to dance, Mishka's fuzzy paws on my hand. Has Polina been the same? Too dazed and confused to know what's real and what isn't? I listen to the noise of Nastya taking off her shoes and chatting to Vitor. She sounds tired, but still as sweet as a bird in the summer morning. She quietens all the negative thoughts that were swirling around the inside of my head. I smile to myself, I'm glad she's here.

'Thank you for inviting me over, Vitor, my family would never have let me walk over by myself,' I hear her chirp.

'It's not a problem, Polina seemed to brighten up when I came over, so,' he trails off. I wonder if he's told them we're supposed to be leaving for Nizhny, or would that be too *soft*? I turn to Babushka, who seems to be staring off into her own little world in the dark corner of the ceiling.

'Babushka,' I whisper sternly, grabbing her attention, 'how do I look?'

She giggles, 'like you've been in bed for three days.'

I panic, I look awful, I feel terrible, and I bet my hair looks horrible. Wait a minute! I lick the inside of my palm, wetting it with my saliva. There's so much of it that the little bubbles form, making my hand feel weirdly soapy. Without thinking, I wipe my wet palm through my hair, like I'd seen Marlen do so successfully at Gertruda's birthday party. I try to slick back the curtains that are starting to form. I can feel the wetness touch my scalp; it doesn't feel nice.

'Better?' I ask again, but she doesn't have time to answer.

'Yuri!' Nastya enters the room, running towards me.

'Nastya!'

She runs over to my bed and gives me a large hug. I breathe in heavily through my nose, taking her all in. I've missed her smell, her clothes feel softer than mine, her presence is so much more pronounced than everybody else in the room. It's a lot of emotion, so much so that my forehead starts to cry.

Wait, why is my forehead crying?

I can feel the oozy saliva dribbling down from my hairline towards my nose. It's okay, no need to panic, I just need to reach my hand around the back of her head so I can wipe it off…

Nastya starts to pull away, 'so Yuri, Vitor says…'

I cut her off by pulling her back in again, squeezing her tighter and causing her to squeak slightly. To my surprise she does the same back, after a brief moment of confused hesitation.

'I'm sorry,' I whisper into her ear, the words leave my mouth much easier than I thought they would.

'It's okay,' she whispers back, causing the knot in my stomach to ease, leaving only the horrible feeling of sickness behind. For a moment I forget about the slobber on my forehead, well, until a chubby thumb squashes into my face, wiping it up into my hairline again.

Nastya pulls out of our embrace and looks behind her with a face of confusion, Vitor is there wiping his hand on his trousers.

'S-sorry,' he stammers, 'I thought I saw a mosquito buzzing around you both.'

'Oh, I didn't hear one?' Nastya says, puzzled.

'Must have been an earwig,' Vitor shrugs, 'I'm going to get a tea, does anyone want anything?'

'Yes please, dear,' Babushka raises her hand far faster than an ill, elderly woman should have. It causes her bones to click.

'Coming right up,' he shoots me a wink before he leaves, this must be what getting along with your older brother feels like.

Nastya perches herself at the foot of my bed, gently creasing the sheets as she sits. When she smiles at me, it's like all the horrible queasiness from the last three days vanishes into a giant puff of smoke, floating out of the window never to be seen again. I open my mouth to speak.

'You kids just pretend I'm not here,' Babushka interrupts, 'I'll just do a puzzle in my book and drink my tea when it gets here.'

I look at Nastya again and giggle, which she does in return. Her face drops after a moment.

'I heard you were going back to Nizhny.'

Looks like Vitor told her after all.

'Papa is making us leave,' well, he actually wanted us to go this morning, but I'm not going to tell her that.

'At least I get to say goodbye,' she touches my arm softly.

'Yeah,' I trail off, 'I'll miss you.'

'I'll miss you too,' our eyes link again. Hers look sodden. More so than my forehead was just moments ago. I can feel Babushka watching us intently, even though she said she wouldn't.

Vitor returns to the room with some tea for Babushka and hands it to her slowly, being careful not to spill it onto her sheets.

He turns back to us, his eyebrows jumping off his face suggestively, 'hey Yuri, reckon you could move over to the other room? I'm sure Nastya would love to see your spaceship before I have to walk her home.'

'I hope that's not a euphemism, dear,' Babushka snaps.

'Babushka, he literally has a cardboard spaceship in the other room,' Vitor sighs.

I have no idea what the pair of them are talking about, but I honestly don't feel too ill compared to this morning, and it has been a few days since I flew it last. With Nastya there, we might even be able to defeat the Moon Force this time.

'Okay, can you help me through?'

'Sure,' Vitor nods.

I sling my arm over his shoulder as he walks me through to the other room gingerly, my stomach starts to gurgle again, but it isn't bad enough to force me back to bed. Even if it was, I'll show Babushka I'm not soft. I eat my eggs in the morning.

Nastya follows us through quietly, probably happy that she doesn't have to stay in that rancid room Babushka and I have inhabited for the last three days. The door to the front room squeaks open and standing there in all its glory is Sputnik 0.5, just as I left it, still slightly torn at the edges from mine and Mishka's last expedition.

'Travelling companion?' Nastya enquires on seeing my creation. She's not in the know about the government project, and it's probably safer if it stays that way. Maybe if the letter arrives in time, I could request a seat for her, it's not like I can fly in my current state anyway. At the moment though, it's better to lie.

'Seemed like a good name for it, especially because without it there's no travelling!' I smile at her, 'maybe today you could be my Sputnik?'

Nastya blushes with a cute smile, her cheeks turning the red of tulips in bloom. My face feels warm just watching hers.

'So, how do we launch it?' She plays with the damaged flaps of my painted cardboard ship.

'Well, we get inside, and then it happens,' I hobble over to the rocket. Vitor has left us alone to go and keep Babushka company. I'm still not quite sure where Mama and Papa have gotten to, the last I saw of them they were arguing over that bottle of vodka. Using all my strength I pull myself over into the ship, Nastya following me inside. I close the hatch, and as if by magic we're at the launch site, the Urals fully in view in front of us, just as they had been the first time I launched Sputnik 0.5.

She gasps, grazing her hands across the ice-cold metal of Sputnik 0.5's iron interior walls. Her eyes fall to the mountains that stand proudly in front of the window.

'Yuri! This is incredible!'

'Isn't it just? I built it all myself!'

'Yourself?!' Another voice catches the pair of us off guard, followed by a slam of the hatch. Mishka crawls down the ladder from the roof.

‘Didn’t think you’d take this baby out without me, did you?’ He says smirking, his one eye fixating on Nastya suspiciously.

I run over and give him the biggest hug. I can’t believe it, first he’d gone and delivered my letter to the government, now he’s entering Sputnik 0.5 in front of Nastya. The matted fur of his paw pulls away from my back, his attention turns back to her.

‘Who’s the new crewmate?’ He asks as though *he’s* the captain.

‘Nastya - from school? I thought I’d show her Sputnik 0.5 before we moved away,’ I scratch the back of my head awkwardly. I’m feeling better, but saying those words out loud brings a different kind of sickness back.

‘Oh yeah, the one you always talk about from school? Is this the girl where you know it's her compared to the other two?’ A sewn-on smile appears on his lips before he laughs.

‘I told you that in confidence,’ I braintalk furiously to him. I know he can hear me, yet he just folds his arms and keeps the smile pasted onto his face. What has gotten into him?

I can feel my face go bright red, that isn’t something that Nastya was ever supposed to hear. I turn on my heel, finding her blushing and confused.

‘I have no idea what he’s talking about,’ the words ooze out of my mouth with the thickness of borscht. The shocked expression on my face doesn't sell my lie particularly well.

'It's okay,' she pushes her hair behind one of her ears, 'I think it's cute.'

A goofy smile grows quickly across my face. I'm unable to stop it spreading as it stretches from ear to ear. I don't know what's gotten into me either, she's just Nastya. She's just a girl, so why do I feel like I can grow wings and fly when I'm around her?

'I'm Mishka. Don't get too comfortable, this thing goes quickly when it launches,' Mishka shoves past me, wiping the pleasant smile from my face. He marches over to the front two seats that look out the window across the Urals. Behind them, the ship has a few seats around some monitors that show the status of Sputnik 0.5's diagnostics. There are about four of them in total. Then, all the way at the back, is another seat facing the cold iron wall. It looks like Mishka has made a lot of changes since our last flight, so many that I'm not sure whether this can actually be classed as Sputnik 0.5 anymore.

'That's your seat,' Mishka points towards the one at the rear, without even glancing at Nastya.

I watch as she twiddles her fingers awkwardly.

'Uhm Mr. Bear, can I sit next to the window please? That chair at the back doesn't have a very good view.'

'No, you might touch something and mess up the launch,' Mishka's attention doesn't move from the bells and whistles he's playing with at the front.

'I promise I won't.'

'Mishka,' I butt in, 'you're being mean.'

'No, I'm not, she'll send the ship off balance - the weight distribution needs to be perfectly even or we're not going to launch properly. Unless you *want* to crash into the mountains? Or give up your own seat at the front?' He chuckles to himself, thinking that I've been beaten.

'Fine,' I say, 'Nastya, you can have my seat, Mishka can show you how all of the controls work.'

His one eye burns like it's been set alight.

'Okay, take your seat then *captain*,' the sarcasm flicks off his tongue.

'Thanks,' Nastya mouths over to me as I buckle-up my seatbelt. She flashes me a thumbs up, the perfect antidote for Mishka's sour words. I take my seat at the back of the cabin, knowing how useless sitting here is, but doing it for Nastya's sake, it isn't her fault that Mishka's acting like a mu-dak. I secure the belt that straps me into my seat and watch as Nastya does the same. Mishka reaches across her, pressing all the buttons and preparing to launch, making sure to stretch over her to make her feel as in the way as possible.

'Everybody buckled up? It's going to be a bumpy ride!' Mishka shouts to the pair of us, before pushing the lever forward with force without warning, sending us flying toward the Urals.

***

The Moon Force isn't here when we break through the atmosphere, giving Sputnik 0.5 a chance to drift through space like a soapy bubble from the washing up tub. Nastya's eyes can't tear themselves from the window, they've seemingly popped out of her head and are scanning every inch of space, absorbing it as though she'd never see it again. The Moon shines brightly, casting her in a light I've never seen before. Mishka just sits with his arms folded, muttering in a bearlike language under his own breath - obviously saying something unsavoury he doesn't want anyone else to hear. I don't know what's gotten into him.

I reach down to my buckle and loosen it, my legs don't take long to start rising from the chair, floating in the most peculiar way. It's like the outer space from behind the windows has managed to get inside, letting me travel through the air.

I grab the back of the chair I'm sitting on and pull myself towards it, letting go and drifting to the front of the cabin at a slow speed. I can't help but stare out of the window as I glide through the ship, the clouds on the Earth's surface seem to be stuck to it, like some sort of gluey fungus, the sort that grows on our potatoes when they've been in the cupboard for too long, or the ones Mama tells me to put back down at the market. She always makes me wash my hands when I get home after something like that, she says it can make me ill. Not that it matters much now. I think about the illness I've felt for the last few days. Though I don't feel unwell at all right now, drifting through the silence of space. No screaming from Mama or Papa, no Vitor tormenting me, no '*There Are So Many Golden Lights*' playing on the radio or Babushka snoring like a wild beast. I come crashing down, literally, as I bump into the back of Nastya's chair - causing her to make an *'oof'* sound as she tears her vision away from the window for the first time since launch.

I close my eyes, anxious that I've ruined her moment, yet her giggle prizes them open, and I'm met with her circling the cabin in the air with me. Her smile takes all of the attention away from the universe around me, her eyes prettier than any solar flare. I close my own eyelids again, savouring this perfect moment.

Mishka lets a sigh escape from his fuzzy mouth. I'm about to comment before the alarm starts blaring, like it did during our last fight with the Moon Force. My eyes snap open, finding Nastya inches from my face, her expression is frantic, like she's floating in a giant sink, and somebody has pulled the plug.

Mine and Mishka's conflict zaps away in an instant.

‘Is it the Moon Force?’ I bark, gesturing Nastya to kindly move away from the chair and to the back, which she does gratefully and with minimal fuss. She retreats to the seat I was in before, attaching herself to it by doing up the buckle. There she sits wide-eyed, diverting her gaze from the windows, in stark contrast to her earlier behaviour.

‘I’m not sure, my scanners are picking up a large object moving our way at enormous speed,’ Mishka plays with the buttons on the dashboard, ‘it might be time to get the new weapons I installed online.’

I know that we’re in danger, but I can’t stop the grin from spreading across my face.

‘You installed weapons? When did you get the chance to do that?’ My voice is far too excited for this situation.

‘There’s the Russian in you,’ my bear laughs, ‘you’ve been in bed for days, you didn’t expect me to sit there on that toy box that whole time, did you?’

Mishka slams his paw into the large red button on the control panel, causing a device to pop out of the desk in front of me. It’s attached by a wire and contains even more buttons than our radio at home. I grab it in both hands, causing a small cannon to poke out of the front of our ship. It moves as I press the buttons. I select the red one on the remote, causing a large beam to shoot out into the cosmos, deafening the alarms that blare through our cabin.

‘Woah,’ I hear Nastya say from the back.

I watch as the beam echoes into space, colliding with a large floating rock and turning it into space dust that will no doubt linger forever. It's not like anyone has a broom up here.

Mishka swats my hand roughly, causing me to retreat.

'Watch what you're doing with that thing, you could accidentally shoot at the Motherland! If you're going to fire at Earth, at least try and get Uncle Sam,' my furry friend laughs.

There's that name again.

I glance out the front window, face to face with us is the largest asteroid I have ever seen. Were it not barreling towards us, I would have mistaken it for another planet.

Me and Nastya scream in unison, my hands pulling away from the weapons device.

'What are you doing? Shoot it! Shoot it!' Mishka screams in my direction, before striking my chair with his leg, sending me spinning across the cabin, floating in every direction except in the way that I want to be looking.

As I spin, I manage to see Mishka shooting the asteroid, yet the beams just absorb into its surface, like a giant laser-absorbing sponge. I let myself spin another half-rotation, stealing a look at Nastya's face. I'm too far away to reach out and comfort her. I finish my spin back to facing the front, catching the moment that the meteorite crashes into the front of the ship, causing a loud and deafening bang. Just like the one that went off outside my window some nights ago, the one that had reduced Vitor to a cowering baby under his blanket, the one that had made me and Babushka so ill, the one that had made Papa run and Mama sob in the doorway.

My eyes burn again as I watch it, unable to tear my gaze away from another explosion. My brain stings like I'm back there watching the mushroom cloud from my bedroom window. I start screaming, my body alights with fresh pain, I start feeling claustrophobic, like I'm tied up with invisible rope that won't let me go. The fire swallows Sputnik 0.5 whole, and then, there's only darkness.

Wednesday 2nd October, 1957.

City 40, Chelyabinsk Oblast, Russian SFSR, Soviet Union.

I wake up tangled in my sheets. The sun sneaks through the window like it's trying to avoid getting caught, yet it still worms its way into my eyes. I've thrown up everywhere, turning my bed into a horrible stew of cotton and red liquid. I look around my room, Nastya isn't here, the last time I saw her she was on the ship. But if I'm here, in my bedroom, then she must be fine too, right? I glance over to Mishka's seat on the top of my toy box, he's still there with his beady eye, watching, as always.

My eyes start to adjust to being awake, I wipe the crust away that has appeared across my eyelids. Mama calls it *sleep*, but why is it called that if it only appears when I'm awake? It's never there in the middle of the night, only in the morning. I turn to look at Babushka's bed, her blankets are a knotty tangle poking upwards towards the sky. I can't see her face on her pillow, yet the crease in its case is still there. As the sun slowly begins to shine through brighter, I can see a stray elderly foot sticking out from the wreckage of her duvet on the floor.

I try to stand, but my stomach returns to feeling like burning water, sloshing around as I move. My face stings like it's been splashed with acid, or rocket fuel even. There's nothing I can do, except...

'Mama…' My voice is hoarse, not much louder than a croak. The view of Babushka's wrinkly foot is scarier than the explosion, than the asteroid, than the Moon Force, than Dimitri or Mikhail, than Mr. Dragunov, or even the vodka that has found its new home in Papa's hands. Where's our Domovoy? Babushka always said he was supposed to protect us from things like this, maybe he doesn't care about us anymore. He's not turned up to help with *anything.*

'Mama…' my frog-like voice grows in volume, still not loud enough to cause a stir. I fight against the fiery sensation that dances across my body, pulling myself to a stand. My knees threaten to buckle, the carpet of my bedroom looks so inviting, like the scent of Nastya's hair. I stumble over, my head twirling like a spinning top. I fall to the side of Babushka's bed, my hands sink into her thin blankets. I peer across her bed, down into the crack between it and the wall. It's then I see her face, mouth open, sideways on the floor, a puddle of coloured drool collecting on the carpet.

The scream that comes out of my lungs is the most painful thing I've ever experienced, but it finally gets my family's attention.

***

Mama tells me that Babushka died last night, during another episode of her dancing tremors. The same ones she'd started the night before last. It seems like she grew tired of waiting for me to join her on the dancefloor and decided to go alone. Mama says that she's in a better place now, one where she isn't hurting anymore. Papa hasn't said anything, the only sound he makes comes from the swill of the bottle as he drinks, it's almost like he can't bear to look at me directly. Everyone keeps apologising that I '*was the one to see her first*', even Vitor, but I don't know what good apologising does, I still see her face every time I close my eyes.

***

Papa closes the door after coming back up the stairs of our apartment block and speaks his first words of the day to everyone.

'They've taken her to the morgue, we'll have to wait a week until the funeral. Apparently, they've been busy the last few days,' his words choke, 'we can't go back to Nizhny yet.'

Papa picks up his half-drank bottle from the table, the liquid inside is a dark red. It's not the clear vodka he's been drinking for the last day or so. I actually think it's the bottle Sanzhar brought with him when he and Alikhan came for dinner.

'I'm sorry,' he stumbles over his words with a slur, 'I need to lie down.'

With that, he staggers off to his bedroom again. The door creaks lazily as it shuts without a slam. Then, there's silence. Mama gathers up the bloody and vomit-covered blankets from mine and Babush... I mean, the spare bed, taking them into the kitchen to scrub them clean. I lay on my sheetless bed, shivering from the cold in my fresh nightgown as Vitor searches the room for extra blankets. My teeth chatter together with the structured rhythm of drums. My brain aches, like it's melting as my body tries its best to freeze over. I look down at my arms, little boils have started to appear, decorating me with polka dots.

'Here we go,' Vitor says, pulling a dusty oversized blanket from the drawer and shaking it out. An army of dust mites fall from the fabric, spraying out in every direction. Vitor lets out a large sneeze as one crawls up into his nose, the dust causes me to cough hoarsely, making my chest feel like it's going to burst open for some other life form to run out across the room. I sigh, coughing reminds me of Babushka.

'Sorry, I didn't realise how dusty it was, but at least it's usable,' he whips the blanket out above me, letting it fall over my body in its warm grasp. The moment it touches my skin, I feel the urge to itch, but at least it's warm. I've gotten used to the itching sensation in my lungs, so it won't take me too long to get used to this either. As I snuggle the blanket into my chin, it causes me to sneeze painfully.

'Maybe don't put that so close to your face, here,' Vitor turns and grabs Mishka from atop the box, 'cuddle into Mishka instead, I know he's your favourite.'

He plops my bear next to my face, I pull him over to me using my chin and rest on him gently, being careful not to catch myself on his single buttoned eye.

My brother coughs heavily into a closed fist, his cheeks puffing out like balloons. He shakes his head and wipes his hand on his shirt. Vitor looks down to me with a look I haven't seen him give me before.

'I used to have a bear as well, you know,' he begins, his voice raspy from his cough.

'Really?' I squeak, genuinely surprised.

'Yeah, I did,' his voice clears as he speaks, 'I brought him with me from Nizhny, you were too young to remember what it was like there, but I remember it so vividly,' he sits at the edge of my bed, letting his hands rest on his chunky belly.

'What was it called?' I ask, the dust in my throat making me sound like an old man.

'Oka, it's the name of the river that flows through the city,' he laughs to himself, 'it's funny, every time Mama talks about me as a child I always wanted to be in that river. Apparently, I used to run off when she wasn't looking, and I'd try and jump in. I even named my bear after it, Mama used to call me…'

'Rybka,' I say without thinking.

Vitor's eyes grow wide, knowing immediately that I'd been awake for their private conversation. The smile falls from his face, not in anger, but though his acting class is over and he's free to be himself again, another mask that has fallen away. After a moment, it's replaced by a genuine smile. He ruffles my hair slightly, being careful not to shake my aching brain underneath.

'I should have known that you were pretending to be asleep, that's on me,' he seems to lose himself in his thoughts after speaking. This isn't the same Vitor I've come to know over the years, this Vitor is soft and kind, whereas the one I grew up with was mean-spirited, nasty and violent. I go to ask him, but almost as though he speaks the same braintalk as me and Mishka, he's already answering.

'I'm sorry you had to hear that conversation Yuri, and I'm sorry for being such an awful brother. I don't know what came over me really, everyone started calling you Mechtatel and said you were going to do all these big things with your life. It was like they'd all forgotten about me, like their Rybka no longer existed. You'd taken Papa's interest in science, Mama's gusto and Babushka just liked you because you were the smallest.'

I wait for him to continue speaking, even though the cough stuck in my throat wants to interrupt his words so badly.

'It made me dislike you, and your bear, and your friends, and your interests. I lashed out because I felt like you were the favourite, because everyone in this house seemed to think that you were the only one of us who could go on and do something important,' he sighs slowly, the well in his eyes beginning to leak.

'It wasn't your fault you were treated that way, and I'm sorry I took it out on you,' he looks out of the window into the cloudy skies across City 40, 'Polina helped me realise all of this.'

Vitor reaches a hand into his pocket, pulling out something in his fist. He opens his palm to show me a small golden butterfly, with crystals of green and red across its wings, its eyes a dark ocean blue. He rolls it around his palm, showing me the pin on the back.

'This is Polina's family brooch,' his breath is short and raspy, 'her mother gave it to me just yesterday, with instructions to give it to Nastya when she's old enough. Do you know what that means?' He asks me, water beginning to fall from his face.

'That she loses things a lot?' I say. Vitor chokes on his words and laughs like I've said something funny. His smile beams at me, he ruffles my hair again.

'Yeah, she can't be trusted. That's why I've asked Mama to take her with us to Nizhny, Nastya I mean.'

'She's coming with us?' My voice breaks with excitement.

'Yeah buddy,' he draws a sharp breath, 'with us…'

'What about Polina? And her mama and papa?' I ask him, his tears have started to form again.

'P-Polina and her parents - they're… going to the same place that Babushka went to Yuri, the same place that…' He's not looking me in the eyes, they're running off like Marlen's usually do.

Mama bursts through the door before he can finish his sentence.

'Vitor. I need you in the kitchen,' her eyes are puffy and red, 'it's your turn to wash the blankets,' she points to the other room sternly.

'But Mama, I…'

'But Mama nothing, Rybka, please.'

His face drops, he cups my face in his hands before planting a kiss on my forehead. This affection he's showing me is more alien than any encounter I've had with the Moon Force.

'Sleep well Mechtatel, I love you.'

He smiles and walks out without looking back, I can hear his sobbing from the doorway. Mama smiles at me.

'I'll go and make you a tea, it'll make you right as rain. Just stay awake for me please Mechtatel or it will go cold. Do you promise?'

'I promise,' I groan, my eyes are feeling so heavy.

'Good, I'll be back shortly,' the door creaks until it shuts tightly.

What's gotten into them? I cuddle closely with Mishka, who's strangely silent. Maybe he's sleeping. The thought of him being asleep makes me tired. Even though I promised Mama that I'd stay awake, I could have a quick nap before my cup of tea arrives, she can just wake me up when she gets back. That's the best of both worlds, a hot tea and a nap. I let my eyelids close.

Shortly after that, I'm gone.

***

'Dance, dance, dance,' Babushka sings from a familiar place. She's back on the same dancefloor as last time, yet instead of the darkness that had surrounded her before, there's now a giant ballroom, with chairs and tables and food from all across the Union. Mishka runs around between her legs, still dancing to the tune of '*There Are So Many Golden Lights*'. It doesn't seem like they play any other songs on the radio here.

'Babushka, look, Yuri's back!' He shouts, causing her to turn and look at me. Her smile is large, genuine and loving. She looks happy and healthy as she moves in time with the beat that plays behind her. I look down at myself, the boils on my arms, the drool that has slipped from my face onto my tatty nightgown is all there. I gaze at Mishka, his second eye is sewn into its socket, his fur seems clean and well-washed. They both wave me over.

'Mechtatel, you can't leave your Babushka waiting, come and dance with us!' She holds out her hand ready to waltz. Mishka runs over to me like he had last time, reaching out for my hand. This time, I accept, and allow him to walk me over to Babushka. The moment I step onto the dancefloor, I relax into a sense of calm. The boils that cover my body recede back into it, the itchiness of my lungs and throat subside, my mind begins to think clearly instead of through the thick fog that has lingered for days.

I walk towards Babushka gingerly, taking her hands, before stepping onto her freshly shined shoes. She moves her feet with me on them, holding me up as we dance. I rest my head onto her belly and listen to her hum the tune of '*There Are So Many Golden Lights*' as we sway gently together.

Thursday 3rd October, 1957.

City 40, Chelyabinsk Oblast, Russian SFSR, Soviet Union.

I wake up with a jolt, not because I've fallen in a dream, but because Papa has clutched my shoulders with his rugged hands, shaking me with excitement about something that couldn't wait until I'd woken up naturally. My eyelids snap open, catching his chaotic and clean-shaven face foaming at the mouth. As soon as he notices my open eyes, he drops me back to my dusty blanket. A cloud of mites bounce into the air, which Papa chooses to ignore, instead he thrusts a letter into my half-awake hands.

I rub my eyes; as my ears begin to wake up I can hear Vitor and Mama screaming happily in the kitchen. I turn to the other bed, there's still no

Babushka, in my morning haze I'd half-expected to see her there. What can they all be so merry about now she's gone? Papa stretches his neck back into my vision, catching me off-guard. My flinch causes me to grip tighter to the envelope that had been forced into my hands.

The early morning sun shines through my open curtains, it looks like Mama just left me sleeping instead of waking me up when my tea was ready. I was looking forward to that.

'Mechtatel! Open your letter!' He points towards my palms giddily.

I don't understand the commotion, it's only a letter. Mama and Papa normally receive post telling them to pay this or pay that. Why are they so happy about this one? I glance down at the rough paper in my hands. It's addressed to me.

The stamp in the top right corner is a dull blue, with a stern looking Lenin shouting at a crowd with a cap in his hands. The hammer and sickle are presented in front of him proudly, the words *Post of the USSR* are brandished across its printed ribbon. There's an illegible black stamp printed across it, blurring some of the other words and making the man's beard look much larger than it actually is. Looking at the return address, my mouth drops agape.

First Secretary Khrushchev
Tsentrosoyuz Building
Moscow
Soviet Union, 101000

I catch Papa's eyes with my own, my body starts to move uncontrollably. I jump into him with a hug, I don't even know what the letter says, I just can't believe that they've responded.

'Has he opened it yet?' Vitor shouts as he comes barrelling through the doorway, followed closely by Mama. The pair of them look so excited, so unaware of Babushka's absence. Something doesn't feel quite right, but I can't put my finger on it.

It's then I become aware of how much better I'm feeling, no pain chewing away behind my eyes, nothing trying to crawl out of my stomach. I glance down at my arms, my boils haven't completely healed, but their redness is beginning to fade, leaving pale blotchy marks where the itching used to be.

'No, he hasn't, he's daydreaming again. Come on Mechtatel, we're all waiting,' Papa squeezes my arm impatiently, before handing me the letter opener he has in his hands. I could have sworn he wasn't holding that a second ago.

Finally, I comply with their wishes, slicing between the gap of the letter and its seal with one movement. I fold the flap back and take out the paper inside, my family gather around behind me to rudely read it over my shoulder.

Dear Comrade Rubinov,

I found the report of your encounter with extra-terrestrial life most concerning. Although we initially planned for the Sputnik 1 project to be an unmanned mission, your reports and experience make you an ideal candidate for a manned launch. Appropriate steps are already being made to attach a cabin to the side of the spacecraft, as well as a defensive weapon for this 'giant claw' you speak of.
There will be five seats on the spacecraft, including yourself, so please assemble an adept crew ready for departure tomorrow for arrival at this address:

Baikonur ⅕, Tyuratam, Kazakh SSR, Soviet Union.

We will send a car for pick up this afternoon at 15 hundred hours. Say hello to your Babushka for me.

His Excellency,

Nikita S. Khrushchev

My heart twinges as I read his greetings to Babushka, she would have been just as over the Moon as I will be tomorrow. My grief can only settle for a moment though, as my family begins celebrating again, picking me up and throwing me in the air. It's a good job that I no longer feel sick, that the dust in my lungs is no longer there, otherwise I wouldn't have been able to cope with being lifted, nevermind boarding a satellite.

Hidden behind the sound of my family cheering, I can hear the radio mumbling in the front room. I can hear it saying my name, about me getting offered a space on the Sputnik 1 launch. But as hard as I try to focus on it, the sound is always out of reach, my family deciding to raise their volume whenever I'm about to hear it properly.

'Mechtatel! You're going to space! You did it!' Mama shouts excitedly, dragging me back from my thoughts.

'Way to go, Yuri!' Vitor joins in.

I watch as a tear rolls down Papa's cheek, that single droplet fills me with so much pride. I can see Mishka sitting in the corner on his toybox, the second eye he had on the dancefloor is gone, leaving him with just the one again. Strangely though, his normal woven scowl is now a bright and brimming smile, as though somebody had resewn him without me looking.

'I knew it would work,' I hear him say to me in braintalk.

‘So, who are you going to take?’ Mama asks, ‘you have five seats, who are you thinking of filling them with? Other than yourself of course.’

‘Definitely his new girlfriend, Nastya,’ Mishka speaks directly into my ear without moving. I frown, he isn’t wrong that I’m going to take her, but calling her my girlfriend is a bit too far. My mind wanders to her moving to Nizhny with us, the thought of seeing her everyday makes my insides dance.

‘I’m guessing Nastya,’ Vitor says, almost as though he’d been part of our conversation.

‘Definitely Marlen as well,’ Mama puts her hand up as she speaks, trying not to be rude.

‘You can’t forget Alikhan,’ Papa is the last to speak. I scratch my head; it seems as though my crew has already been picked for me. That leaves only one more spot on the ship.

‘Do you know who the last one will be, Mechtatel?’ Mama asks.

‘That’s easy,’ my eyes glance to the other side of the room, ‘my last crew member will be…’

‘Dimitri? Mikhail?’ Vitor says with a smirk.

‘Absolutely not, I’m taking Mishka!’ I fling my finger towards him as he sits on his toybox throne, my family glance around at each other confused.

‘You’re the captain, Mechtatel,’ Papa says, purposely avoiding my gaze, ‘I thought you’d have left room on the ship for…’ his pause fills the room.

'Poschekotat' Ruku!' He barks, grabbing my entire chest with his big hairy hand and tickling me. I can't help but scream, a howl escapes my lips as I try to tear him off me. Mama and Vitor laugh together. The volume dies down after a while, leaving the room in silence again.

'Anyway, the cup of tea you asked for should be brewed, I'll bring it through for you now,' Mama potters off to the other room to gather it for me.

I knew I'd be able to get away with a quick nap before she brought it through, I didn't have to promise anything to her after all. Here I am, well-rested, healthy, going on a government mission into space and waiting for a cup of sweet tea from Mama. Things couldn't be any better, except for Babushka still being here of course.

Wait, I look out of the window again, isn't it the next morning?

***

The car horn outside beeps, echoing around my bedroom. I've spent the last hour or so packing my rucksack with Mama, making sure to remember all my essentials: clothes, toiletries, some books, my spinning tops, my toy digger, some crayons and paper and Mishka of course - although he won't be travelling inside the suitcase, he'd be too cramped inside there, and he's got his own seat anyway.

I hug Papa, his eyes well with delight - he can't believe I'm going to space, and being honest, I can't believe it either.

'You're making the Rubinov family proud, Mechtatel,' he says as he pulls me close, getting all of his soppy tears all over the nice shirt Mama made me wear.

'I'm so proud you inherited my love of science, my boy,' I think he would have gone on forever if Mama didn't tear him away from me. The car outside honks again, speeding up my goodbyes.

'Come back safely to me,' Mama says as she hands me a paper bag, 'I know the drive to the Kazakh SSR is long so I packed some pelmeni for the drive, I wouldn't want my little space explorer getting hungry,' she squeezes my cheek so hard that it could have turned it to leather, before placing a big sloppy kiss on the middle of my forehead and letting go.

I take the bag gratefully, peeking into the top to catch a glimpse of Mama's famous dumplings, trying my best to figure out what filling they have inside.

'They're beef and onion,' she chirps.

She must have caught me looking.

'Thank you,' I cuddle into her belly. The car horn echoes around our apartment again, the driver of the vehicle seemingly growing impatient.

I turn to Vitor, who's holding out a hand toward me, waiting for me to shake it. I reach mine forward, only for him to pull it away, placing a thumb on his nose and letting his fingers dance wildly, his tongue sprawls out of his mouth jokingly. I cackle with laughter.

'Come here will you,' he bundles me into a hug, his flabby body like a soft pillow as it swallows me whole. I can't believe this is really my brother.

'You're lucky Polina is feeling much better today, otherwise I might have been upset that you weren't taking me,' Vitor punches me lightly in the arm with a smirk. I hope he knows that even though he's acting nicer, it's going to take a lot more than a few days of brotherly love to make it onto my space travel list. After all, it's still his fault that Mishka has to experience the trip with one eye.

The horn of the government car beeps again, the sound is longer and more drawn out this time. I kiss my family goodbye one last time before I run down the stairs of our building, Mishka bouncing off the steps with me - as though he's trying his best to catch his footing. The pelmeni jumps around the paper bag in my other hand, my rucksack sways on my back under its own weight.

'Make us proud son!' I can hear Papa shout from the doorway.

With their blessing ringing like bells in my ears, I leave them behind to go on my journey.

***

I burst out the doors and into the fresh air of City 40.

Everyone's outside again; playing with their friends, taking walks, shopping. It's funny how a couple of days can change everything. My eyes catch sight of the foamy-mouthed dog that roams around our apartment complex; even he's playing with the children who normally stay as far away from him as possible, the dog is almost smiling with delight at finally being played with.

The sun shines onto my face, warming me up to the point where I start to feel uncomfortable under the jacket Mama made me wear, but thanks to carrying Mishka and my pelmeni, I don't have any spare hands to take it off. Part of me wishes I could grow another arm just to act as a coat rack. Despite the incredible urge to sweat, it's nice to finally be outside again, in a City 40 just as I remembered it before the explosion.

My vision falls to the car in front of our building, it looks like an object that has fallen from space. Its colour is a light blue like the sky on a clear day, the headlights wide and circular as though they're going to start blinking. The bar on the front makes it look like it has fangs, the slice of white that cuts through the paint on the side ending in a red point - the word *Motul* written on the side.

I instantly forget about the heat as I gaze inside, there's a man in a green suit with a matching-coloured hat, across it sits a red band with the Soviet emblem on it. KGB. The officer isn't wearing the stern facial expression that normally comes with the uniform; instead, he looks exhausted as he watches Marlen continuously beep the bright white wheel on the inside. A blue vein on his head pulses thicker every time the horn blares. The shadow that falls from the underside of his hat makes it difficult to make out his face, but I can see a large black moustache living above his lip like an oversized slug.

'Master Rubinov,' the officer starts, 'thank the stars you're here, now we can proceed to collect your other cadets,' he almost sounds thankful to move on.

'You can get in the back now you little brat,' he snarls at Marlen.

'Yuri can get in the back,' my friend retorts with the attitude he always has. The officer's face nearly pops as it grows red; the vein by the side of his ear threatening to burst.

'I'll show you where the crawfish spend the winter[26],' he snaps, picking Marlen up from the seat and throwing him into the back with a thud. The honking stops, the ears of everyone in the area thank the officer kindly.

'Hey! What was that for?' Marlen crosses his arms, before settling into a sulk.

The KGB officer turns to me, 'please, get into the car young man, before me and your friend end up killing each other,' he peers over his shoulder at

---

[26] Russian idiom. To teach someone a lesson.

Marlen as he gets comfortable in his new seat, 'and do me a favour, don't bring him back.'

The officer gets out of the car and helps me take the rucksack off my back, placing it into the back of the car. I open the door and get into the front passenger seat, placing Mishka on my lap for him to look around out of the windows. The officer's chair shakes as Marlen plants a kick into the back of it. The moustached man groans loudly as he gets back into the car.

'Don't listen to him,' Marlen moves his feet to rest at the top of the man's seat, poking into the back of his head, 'is it true that we're all going to space? That's insane - all because of that little box you painted in your living room?'

I nod, I can't quite believe it either, a smile paints across my face. I open the paper bag of beef and onion pelmeni as the officer starts the car. My mind settles as we pull away, until I realise. Why is Marlen already here? I haven't told anyone about my choices for the crew other than my family. My face starts to scrunch, I go to open my mouth and ask the question.

'Is that your Mama's? Her pelmeni is the best,' Marlen bundles into the front and yanks one out of the bag, completely throwing off my train of thought, before throwing himself back to where he was sitting and chewing on it quietly.

I don't get a moment to catch up to my thought train as it barrels down the track, everyone seemingly talking over me as I try to think.

'I thought he'd never shut up,' the officer quips.

'Yeah, just give him the bag for the journey,' a familiar gruff voice says aloud. I can't hide my surprise as I look down at Mishka's mouth moving freely, the sewing that had once kept him quiet is no longer there. He's making a habit of getting up and moving around after delivering my letter. Mishka makes his way to his furry feet and takes the bag of pelmeni in both paws, offering it up to the agent.

'Do you want one before I give it to him?' My eyes shoot from my bear, to the officer, and back to Mishka again. The man hasn't even looked up from the road, until he notices the movement.

'Sure, thanks,' he says, before popping one into his mouth and continuing the drive towards the next stop.

'Can I get another one?' Marlen breaks his silence. Mishka passes him the bag, which he takes without thanks. He turns his one beady eye towards me, then a look of guilt splashes across his face.

'I'm sorry, I just gave all your pelmeni away! I didn't even realise!'

I don't know what shocks me more, the fact he's walking and talking again; or the fact that nobody in this car seems to bat an eyelid that he's doing so. I clench my hands into fists and rub my eyes, in the darkness the stars that I'd seen in space appear - yet every time I look at them through my closed lids they vanish back into darkness, hiding in the corners where I'm not looking. I pull my hands away and open them again, the car has stopped and Mishka's sitting on my lap again, his head slanting like it normally is when he's sitting on top of my toybox, watching the world around him freely.

I follow his eyes and see Alikhan at the side of the road, a massive suitcase weighing heavy in his scrawny hands. Sanzhar stands behind him, peeking into the car suspiciously. The KGB officer gets out of the car to help Alikhan with his heavy suitcase, his Papa seemingly unwilling to assist.

Alikhan waves as he sees me in the front.

'Hi Yuri!' his voice is muffled thanks to the glass of the window. He allows the man to pick up his suitcase and follows him around to the back.

Sanzhar approaches where Mishka and I are sitting, tapping on the window slowly. Marlen doesn't seem to notice; he's still chowing down on *my* pelmeni.

I roll down the window slowly, Sanzhar leans into the car, taking a big look around.

'So, space, ay?' He tuts, 'you're lucky I worked on that project, or I wouldn't be trusting Alikhan to go…' he squeezes his fingers together, as if making a mental log of something.

'Make sure you all take lots of notes for that little ship of yours, we wouldn't want all of that data going to waste,' he backs away from the car when he hears the thud of the closing boot. The uniformed agent returns swiftly, his eyes unmoving from the Kazakh man. Alikhan gives his papa a large hug and gets inside.

'See you soon!'

'And you son - remember we're moving when you get back,' he waves as the car pulls away. Alikhan sits swaying his feet to a rhythm that plays in his own head. Marlen being distracted really does make this process faster.

'Last stop - Nastya,' the officer announces to nobody in particular.

'You're moving?' I ask Alikhan, he turns his head to face me.

'Yeah, I guess so, Papa only told me after the letter from the government came. Apparently, we're leaving the Union for good…' he tails off quietly, most likely because of the peering officer in the rear-view mirror who is watching him carefully.

Wait, why did he get a letter? What's…

'Oh, yes? Where?' The KGB officer's voice spikes loudly, as if he's suddenly become very interested.

'Still in the Bloc. Papa's been offered a job in East Germany. He says he's going to be a science professor, at the University in Leipzig' Alikhan chirps.

The thought of him moving to East Germany makes me think of Yakov, the son of Red Joe that Babushka had loved so dearly. I look at Alikhan, the colour on his face seems to fall in a strange way, darker in areas that shouldn't have been.

'Interesting, and he told you that this morning out of the blue?' The officer says.

'Sure did. I'm so happy for him. We only just moved here though, so I'm going to have to pack up all of my things for a second time. That and make new friends all over again,' he sighs as his eyes wander out of the car window.

I know how he feels, when we return from space, I'll be packing up to move back to Nizhny. Well, at least I think I am, nobody has mentioned it since I woke up this morning, and City 40 seems a lot livelier than it has been for days, not to mention Polina is feeling better so Nastya won't be coming with us even if we are moving. I hope Papa changes his mind so we can stay.

'How peculiar,' the officer says before drifting into silence as we pull up to Nastya's house. Polina is there with her, hugging her tightly.

'And watch out for asteroids this time!' I hear her say, my window still unwound from speaking with Sanzhar.

'Polina, please, they're here,' Nastya's face has turned the colour of a ripe tomato. She must have told her about the crash on Sputnik 0.5, I wonder if she mentioned the Moon Force.

'And you'd better show that Moon Force who's boss if they show up!' Polina pumps her fist in the air.

Yeah, she has.

As he had done with the rest of us, the officer gets out and helps her pack up, before opening the door for her to climb inside.

'Me and Rybka will be listening out for you all on the radio, make us all proud!' She says as she waves us off, Nastya and the others respond with their own waves. I can't bring myself to, too confused over why she knows that name. I thought Vitor's nickname was only known by the family, I only learned of it yesterday, surely he wouldn't have mentioned it to her? Right?

***

The car sputters across the fields of Chelyabinsk Oblast as we drive across the pebbly roads. I was too young when we left Nizhny to remember much of it, only flashes of the town, our old apartment and a little bit of the river after Vitor mentioned it yesterday. Despite searching my memory I've never been able to remember the drive to City 40, so this feels like my first ever journey outside of the city limits, other than going to space in Sputnik 0.5 of course. But going upwards doesn't really count, does it? It's almost like I've been trapped here for years without realising.

Papa told me about the checkpoint that we had to cross in order to get into the city, that all the way around us there are large, barbed wire fences keeping us in like chickens. He told me it wasn't made to keep us in, but to keep everybody else out. I've never understood why we'd want to keep the world out, our city is normal enough, the only thing special about it is Mayak, the radio factory, which has now blown up, so surely nobody wants to come inside anymore?

As we drive up to the gate to leave the City 40 limits, I can see countless men dressed similarly to our driver, yet compared to them, the officer in our car seems much more important. It's only then that I see the medals decorating his chest, and as we pull in closer to stop, that the other men don't have any. Their clothes are baggier and seemingly unironed, compared to the strictly worn uniform of our driver. They also don't stand up very straight, with many leaning on the fences, walls and gates. The men all seem to stiffen as our car approaches, as though the car barked for them to stand at attention without the sound of its horn.

The checkpoint is small and dingy, the barbed wired building to the side of the gate looks like an old convenience store that has been taken over by the military. A man inside the little hut before us grows increasingly rigid as we approach, the smile falling from his face gradually, almost at the same speed as our car. The man in the driver's seat winds down his window.

'Captain Dragunov, Sir, have you retrieved the packages?' The guard says as he stands at attention, his hand glued to his forehead. Wait, what? It's only then that I look at the man's face who has been driving us, the shadow his hat had cast suddenly vanishes as if by Rasputin's magic. It's Mr. Dragunov, the features of his face, his trademark moustache, it's all so obvious now.

A strange squeak comes from one of the backseats as Marlen realises the error of his ways, he's been kicking the back seat of the scariest teacher at school. The rumours were true, he really is KGB, checking up on all of the students for the government. My blood turns to ice. Marlen drops the endless bag of pelmeni to the floor, Nastya and Alikhan sit in awkward silence, having never been on the receiving end of his wrath before.

'At ease, comrade,' Mr. Dragunov says, before turning to us.

'I was wondering how long it would take you troublemakers to realise it was me,' he turns to face the uncomfortable mess named Marlen in the backseat, 'especially you, you little soplyak[27].'

You could slice through the awkwardness in the car with a butter knife.

---

[27] Punk.

'I've got them all with me, it's going to be full speed to Baikonur to make it before the launch tomorrow. Keep an eye on the perimeter, don't let anybody in or out after me,' he turns to Alikhan and smiles before facing the officer again sternly, 'City 40 might have a rat problem.'

'Yes, Sir,' the man in the hut responds, opening the gate and allowing our car to drive through.

'There was a rat that always used to get into our pantry,' Marlen starts nervously, 'it used to nibble little holes in our bags of flour and would eat the paper labels off the tinned food, so we didn't know what was inside. My Mama used to say our dinner was like gambling, or roulette. Until my Papa cornered it one day and smashed it with his bat.'

'That's precisely why the area needs securing,' Mr. Dragunov responds calmly, 'to stop… those sort of rat problems.'

Marlen chuckles awkwardly, before sinking into his seat as low as he could get, obviously wishing it would swallow him whole.

I still can't process why he's here. I look down at Mishka who shrugs his furry shoulders.

Mr. Dragunov seems to sense my, and everyone else's apprehension, opening his mouth to answer a question I never asked.

'I've been watching the school for a number of years, for unique young talent that can benefit the military. I had thought my search was fruitless, until I bumped into Mikhail Vasilyev who'd heard about you getting the government address from Mrs. Palakova of all people,' he scoffs loudly, yet nobody responds to his ramblings. His face falls flat once more as he carries on.

'Well, she refused to tell me anything other than what you were working on was top secret, and that you were planning on approaching the government about being part of the space program.'

I can't quite believe what I'm hearing, yes, I've seen the Moon Force, I'd fought against them and flown amongst the stars in Sputnik 0.5. But despite all of that hard work, I can't believe I have Mikhail Vasilyev to thank for this opportunity. For once, him being a slushatel has actually worked in my favour.

It's then that the thought dawns on me, one that I hadn't dug deeper into before. *I've just been playing.* As much as I pretended that I was flying up to space with Mishka, and meeting aliens and dodging asteroids, I'd just been sitting in a cardboard box in our living room, none of it was real. It's never been real.

I glance up at Mr. Dragunov, he's examining me. My face has given me away, just like it always does when I'm daydreaming.

'What's wrong boy?' He pesters.

'Nothing, I… I just thought that I was playing games at home, with my friends and my bear. Wasn't it all just pretend? You know, Sputnik 0.5?'

Mishka frowns at me with his one eye, like it's the single most offensive thing I've ever said out loud.

'Oh no, what you were doing in your living room was valuable research,' Mr. Dragunov's voice is unnaturally chipper to what I'm used to, 'listen, it's a long drive to Baikonur. You should get some shut eye, like the rest of your friends.'

He'd changed the conversation at staggering speed, and his tone had caught me off guard, more than when he used to scream like an officer at school. It's put me in a position where I feel uncomfortable to ask for further information, despite my longing for answers.

I glance around the car, it's true. Everyone else is flat out asleep, it's just me, Mishka and Mr. Dragunov left awake.

'Oh, before I forget,' Mr. Dragunov begins talking, 'What Marlen says isn't true, they won't throw you in the gulag for wanting to wear a dress. He doesn't even know what one is.'

I smile softly, before my eyes widen in shock.

'Y-you can braintalk?'

'You didn't think it was just you and your bear, did you? Stupid boy,' he laughs.

I suddenly feel heavy, as though Mishka, curled up on my lap, has suddenly turned to iron. My eyes grow dreary, my body crying out for sleep suddenly, my mouth too tired to answer his venomous question.

'Don't worry about me, I can keep myself company on the drive,' he plays with the tiny radio next to the wheel of the vehicle, causing static to fill the car. After playing with the knob for a while, a song finally starts to play, '*There Are So Many Golden Lights*'.

'I enjoy this song, but the lyrics are a bit crass don't you think? But boy, doesn't it make you want to stand up and dance, dance, dance,' he whistles along to the accordion that floats through the song. My drowsy mouth lets his question go unanswered, preferring the car to fall into silence. The only sound I can hear on the drive to the Kazakh SSR is Babushka's song.

Friday 4th October, 1957.

Baikonur ⅕, Tyuratam, Kazakh SSR, Soviet Union.

The drive to the Kazakh SSR doesn’t take as long as I thought it would have, nor does reaching the inside of the facility. As much as I try to think about our journey inside the building, I can't recall anything from my memory. The room I’m in is brighter than any I can ever recall being inside, it’s that synthetic type of light, overcompensating for the lack of windows on any of the walls. There’s just one doorway with a grey handle. The white of the walls makes the room feel even stranger, as does the large white table in the middle.

In front of the door stands Mr. Dragunov, seemingly guarding it from anyone coming in from outside - his green uniform is much brighter in this odd room we find ourselves in. He isn't smiling, nor does he look disgruntled. He's carrying the look of a man at work who is ready to call it a day and go home to bed. I look for my friends, but I can't see any of them sitting around the table - Mishka is the only *person* I recognise, and he's sitting right next to me, staring at the other *people* around the table with his frosty eye.

I glance over to where he's looking, around us, three men stare in our direction, seemingly waiting for us to speak. They all look peculiar in their own ways.

I know the first man from the posters stuck up across City 40. It's Chairman Khrushchev. From here he looks podgy and soft, with wisps of balding white hair that seem like they'll float away if he doesn't run his hands across his scalp often. As if on cue, he licks his hand and rolls a sweaty palm across his head, sticking the strands back into their place. He smiles towards me as he notices my inspection, a gap between his two front-teeth becomes visible, large enough you could roll a ruble between them if you aimed it right. In the chair next to him is a beige-coloured stuffed bear, not much taller than Mishka, but who still has both of his eyes. The bear wears a red beret that leans to the side, a Soviet emblem brandished across it.

Across from him is an old white man with a long wispy beard and a top hat, a blue banner and stars are painted across it. He wears a large red bowtie and a blue coat, he seems to have a permanent frown scribbled onto his face alongside his wrinkles, as though he's taking something very seriously. The man seems to be incredibly sweaty, as if he's the only one in the room that can feel the heat. Beside him, is a fuzzy and cute looking stuffed bear, with a slight centre parting for hair. The bear wears small, circular glasses and seems to be rummaging through some notes.

Lastly, directly in front of me, is a man who glistens a bright red colour. His skin, his hair, his clothing all different shades, like he's been pulled directly out of a government poster. He's a scowling man with a thick moustache that makes Mr. Dragunov's look like the facial hair of a teenager. The man wears a budenovka[28] with a star on it that covers his hairline. I can feel his gaze on me like a heavy weight, the pipe that hangs from his mouth threatens to fall to the table as its smoke drifts into the air. Another stuffed brown bear sits next to him, its body language shy and nervous, like it's trying to look everywhere but toward the others sitting at the table. Unlike everyone else, the bear lacks any remarkable clothing or features. Even compared to Mishka and his missing eye.

I turn back to Mishka and use my brain to talk to him.

---

[28] A distinctive hat worn by many members of Soviet military.

'Mishka, who are these people?'

He turns his head to respond, yet before he can, Khrushchev speaks up loudly, sounding exactly as he does on the radio, complete with crackly static and everything.

'We're the people sending you into space little one, I'd appreciate it if you spoke to the room,' he smirks at me, causing his chins to press together. The other men and bears around the table laugh, except the one who looks like he doesn't want to be here.

The red man's hand slams into the table and shoots it daggers.

'Yakov, can't you even bring yourself to laugh? Are you that much of a disappointment that your own mouth doesn't work? I don't even know why you're here - stupid mu-dak,' he tuts loudly, unclenching his fist and taking a long drag of his tobacco pipe.

The sweating man with the top hat points at me with a straight finger, 'don't you pay no mind to Red Joe y'hear? He's just angry because y'all are the ones on the spaceship,' he retrieves his hand and ruffles the hair of the spectacled bear next to him, 'how's the math, Teddy?'

'So, we've attached a sidecar to Sputnik 1 for you and your crew to inhabit, it'll be a tight squeeze but it'll comfortable enough for you all,' Teddy the bear plays with his glasses to read the words correctly, his other paw struggles to keep the papers straight on account of having no usable thumbs. The hatted man uses one of his hands to hold them up for him as he scans across the pages, leaving a moist mark where his thumb presses down.

'We haven't been able to detect any alien life or this Moon Force you speak of, but we've attached a cannon on the underside of Sputnik 1, just in case it's needed...'

The beige bear with the beret speaks up, 'Sam, can you muzzle your beast? It seems to think it's in charge of a Soviet operation,' he leans back in his seat with his fuzzy arms folded, waiting for the fireworks.

'I don't see where your notes are Suez, if this was up to you it would end up a crisis,' Teddy splutters with a snap.

'I don't need notes to tell him that we've picked a perfect time for lift-off, and that there's a zero-percent chance of an asteroid collision like his last flight into the LEO. So, he's got nothing to worry about, and neither do you,' the bear named Suez tilts his beret over his eyes lazily, as if to say he's finished talking.

'Stop it - all of you,' Khrushchev's crackling voice snaps, commanding the attention from the table once more, even Yakov musters up the strength to look at him.

'We are about to embark on humanity's greatest adventure, it is true we were beaten to it by this young boy, but now he has our backing there's no stopping us from reaching the final frontier,' he turns to me and Mishka, 'our Sputnik 1 probe has been fitted with state-of-the-art photo technology, what we want is photos of the Earth. Can you do that for us?'

'O-of course,' I stammer, finally finding the strength to speak.

'Say it with more passion boy, we're not sending Yakov into space,' Red Joe raises the back of his hand to his bear, causing it to cower behind its own paws.

'For Mother Russia!' I bellow.

'He's as Russian as the Oka River,' Suez says without opening his eyes.

'Go and get your crew arranged, this will be your last afternoon on Earth before you depart. You've got a big evening ahead of you, young man. The world will be watching,' Chairman Khrushchev stands to his feet and pats me on the back, filling me with an immense sense of pride. If only Babushka was here to see this.

I stand to my feet, lifting Mishka up with me and placing him on my shoulder like a parrot. He leans on my head as though it's the arm of a comfortable chair.

'Farewell Captain Mechatel, Lieutenant Mishka - enjoy this evening, for it may be your last,' Khrushchev's eyes well with pride as he speaks.

Mr. Dragunov walks toward us and guides us out the door, leading us away from the strange table with the stranger men and their stuffed toys. He salutes us as we exit, before closing the door behind us.

The door hasn't been closed for more than two seconds when Mishka decides to open his once sewn together mouth.

'How come you get to be captain?'

I don't respond to his question, too caught up on how the Chairman of the Union knows my family nickname.

***

Walking into the dormitory we'd been given at Baikonur, we find Marlen and Alikhan holding two large pillows tightly, swinging them at each other with all of their might. Feathers float through the air, being blown around frantically the more the pair of them swing their weapons. I still don't quite understand why we've been given a bedroom when we're leaving on the satellite in a matter of hours, but this is the government and who am I to question their practices.

Nastya is sitting on one of the bunkbeds, trying her best to ignore the noise and read her book. She's trying to read '*The Little Gold Key or the Adventures of Buratino*' by Aleksei Tolstoy, it's the same copy that Babushka used to read me before bed when she wasn't too tired, with the exact same tear in the top right corner.

I don't have a chance to focus too hard on it, after a moment I find myself on the floor staring up at the ceiling, knocked over by the force of two feathery pillows to the face.

'Oh no, Alikhan! You killed him!' Marlen gasps, pointing the finger towards the Kazakh. My hazy vision follows his finger to the face of Alikhan, who has turned the colour of pomegranate seeds.

'It wasn't just me Marlen, plus you're the one who's been hitting harder. Not to mention you started it!'

'Shut up, pridurok[29]!'

'You shut up!'

'Both of you shut up,' Nastya pushes between the two of them, knocking them both off balance, 'you could at least help him up instead of squabbling.'

She reaches a sturdy hand towards me that I take gratefully. Nastya hoists me up with a strength I didn't know she possessed, it's as though she's a person-sized ant who can lift much more than her own weight. Now on my feet, I turn on my heel to grab Mishka from the ground, only to find him gone. Looking up again, I can see him jumping up and down on a lower bunk.

'Yeah, this one's just right.' he says whimsically, before laying his head on the pillow that isn't too hard, or too soft.

Alikhan and Marlen are still too busy arguing to notice Nastya has pulled me to my feet, their ever-rising voices causing my already spinning head to

---

29 Moron.

rotate faster; that is, until she takes my hand, causing the spinning top that is my brain to stop in its tracks.

'There's a balcony, do you want to go and see what we can spot from there?' She chirps like a bird in spring. I can't control my head as it nods in agreement, before I follow her out of the heavy metal door.

The wind doesn't hit my face like I had expected it to. We're high up on the building, surrounded by miles and miles of wasteland - bar this building, a few other small ones with towers and the launch pad for Sputnik 1 itself. I can see the smooth surface of its metal from here, all four of its antennae poking out like singular blades of wheat. Our cabin has already been welded to it, a small box-shape with windows. It's then I realise how large the satellite is, much bigger than Papa and Sanzhar had described - possibly because they need more space to fit us in? From this angle I can't see the cannon that Teddy had been talking about, hopefully we won't have to use it, but as long as it's there I can rest easy.

It's around five o'clock in the afternoon, even though the Sun has begun its descent towards the ground again, it's still some way off going to sleep for the night. The Moon won't replace it in the sky for another few hours, but the light is fading lazily across the wasteland around Baikonur, leaving it looking sparser and more barren than it would have in the bright sunshine.

Nastya leans on the white railing of the balcony after closing the door over all the noise, leaving the scenery as ours to witness alone. Our shared sky seems to realise it's just us watching, becoming more dramatic as shades of red and purple dart across the clouds. It's a great evening for shepherds, for a space launch, and for us.

I join her in leaning on the rail, her big grey eyes attached to the sky above.

'I swear life is so much quieter when I'm with Katarina and Gertruda,' she laughs slightly after seeing the door had closed fully, not like those three inside would have been interested enough to listen in anyway.

'Really? These guys might be crazier, but it's those two who don't shut up with their talking,' I try to joke, but her face has dropped, not even registering what I'd said. Her eyes look uninterested, like there's a battle going on behind them, or her heart is warring with the skin that keeps it contained. I can tell words are dancing on the tip of her tongue, and she's unsure whether to say them, or to swallow them forever.

'A-are you excited?' She asks me hesitantly, seemingly having come to a conclusion with her thoughts.

'Of course, we're going to space,' I follow her line of sight. She's watching the clouds float deliberately across the sky, like they're drifting to a tune so lovely and slow.

'Yeah, I know that,' her fingers tap the rail gingerly, 'doesn't it scare you though?'

The question takes me by surprise, 'I don't think so, we've been into space before.'

'No Yuri, we've played rockets in your front room while you were sick. This is different, this is real,' Nastya allows her head to touch the cold of the railing, trembling slightly as she takes in breath.

It's something that's been playing on my mind too. The government has invited us to be part of the Sputnik 1 project thanks to a cardboard rocket in my living room that my one-eyed stuffed bear had sent them a letter about once I'd fallen asleep, after being tipped off by Mikhail Vasilyev of all people. Now here I am talking with world leaders and their own stuffed bears, on the verge of being one of the first people in space.

'They must see something in us, or they never would have invited us to take part,' I place a hand on her shoulder awkwardly, the last thing I want is for her to start crying.

She starts crying, not too hard that she's sobbing, but just enough to register a whimper. Forgetting about my awkwardness, I pull her in for a hug, she returns it with a tight squeeze. I know that she's crying, and that I'm consoling her, but for me it's one of those moments that I don't want to end. Part of me feels awful for feeling that way, wanting a memory of someone suffering to last for eternity, forever on replay like a stuttering radio. But we're close, and it feels like the most natural thing in the world. I feel truly wanted, no adult telling me what to do, or where to go, or forcing a hug on me because we're related. I'm close with someone that I want to be close with, and it fills my stomach with gold butterfly brooches.

'I understand, and I know what you mean,' I pull away slightly, letting the feeling I wanted to experience forever end suddenly.

'You do?' Her eyes meet mine.

'Yeah, it's all very sudden, and not to mention confusing,' I pull at my collar awkwardly, 'and after all, I did pick you to come with me, so I hope you enjoy the trip, otherwise I'll feel terrible for the rest of my life,' I laugh at myself, she flashes me a teary smile but says nothing else.

'And hey, a problem shared is a problem halved right?' I say somewhat confidently, shocking myself. She squeezes my hand gently.

'You've been listening to the radio too much!' She laughs at me, 'is that a line from a serial?'

I feel my face grow red, at least I've been able to make her feel better, even if it's at my own expense, it's definitely worth it. We stand there awkwardly for a moment until the door squeaks open. I look for the person that opened it, unable to find one until I look down towards the ground. Mishka is standing there, his fur fuzzier than usual, a few pillow feathers stuck to his body.

'The big guys are telling us it's time to get suited up, are you ready?'

I glance at Nastya, her grey eyes show no sign of the tears that had once strolled down her face.

'Ready as I'll ever be,' she frowns towards my bear, before her face beams at me.

'Nastya,' Mishka starts, catching her attention again, 'I just want to say sorry for how I was the last time we went up to space together. I don't know what got into me, I think I'm just used to having Yuri to myself. It won't happen again, I'll be better this time,' he ends by smiling a genuine smile, I can't help but give him one too.

She seems taken aback by his apology, taking a moment to steady herself.

'That's okay Mr. Bear, but you can sit at the seat at the back this time,' she chuckles, before letting me go and walking out of the door - making sure to ruffle the fur on Mishka's head as she leaves.

She turns back before she walks through the door properly, 'I'm just kidding, you're the one who knows how to drive.'

Nastya giggles and carries on through to where Marlen and Alikhan are suiting up excitedly, seemingly forgetting their beef over pillows.

The warmth of her hand lingers on mine for a moment, before slowly disappearing and leaving my palm lonely and cold. I raise both hands to my face, rubbing it gently so as to not catch my eyes. Even

Mishka has a smile on his face after his interaction with her.

'Mishka, I think I might have a crush on Nastya,' I blurt out, quietly enough so she can't hear me.

'Don't tell me you've only just realised, mu-dak. I think everyone else has known for ages. You really are a Mechtatel, aren't you?'

My face goes red again.

'Come on Casanova, before they take all the good suits.'

***

The inside of Sputnik 1 is much bigger, flashier, and more high-tech than that of Sputnik 0.5. The cockpit is a shimmering silver, like the water's reflection on a sunny day at Lake Karachay. Inside there are lights, buttons, and switches that all shine different colours of the rainbow, almost blinding us all with how bright they are.

I look over to Nastya, the sunlight that's beginning to disappear on the horizon shines across the wasteland in front of us and through the glass of Sputnik 1's front window. The angle of the light, and the glass, causes a small rainbow to appear on her cheek, as though every single flashing light from the cabin is staring at her like I am. It makes me strangely jealous.

'This is so exciting,' Marlen pulls on the belt that ties him to his chair vigorously, like he's waiting for his dinner to arrive. I hope the government has packed food; I think to myself at the thought of it. Marlen is a pain at the best of times - yet he's an absolute beast when he's hungry.

The real stuffed beast sits in the chair next to me, talking to Alikhan who's sitting behind him.

'So does all of the KSSR look like this dead wasteland?' Mishka asks cheekily.

'Of course it doesn't, I don't think they'd build any pretty housing or statues in a place that's supposed to be secret, do you?' The Kazakh frowns, mainly because of what Mishka said, but partly because of the sun shining directly into his eyes.

'Well, I didn't know, that's why I was asking,' Mishka scoffs.

'Tyuratam is a much more beautiful place than City 40, for starters it isn't a prison that people aren't allowed into.'

'Then why did they let you in?' Mishka probes.

'Grrr… Yuri, shut your bear up will you?'

I go to open my mouth, but a large black box with a speaker interrupts me before I can start speaking.

'Spaceteam Rybka - are you all set for launch?'

My ears twitch to the sound of that name.

'Whoever decided to call us Spaceteam Rybka needs to be fired,' Marlen remarks, becoming bored with the seatbelt that is trying its best to squeeze all the air from his body.

'I think it's because we're going to be exploring the *great ocean* that is outer space,' Mishka says as he toys with the buttons on the control pad, seemingly knowing what he's doing.

'Doesn't mean it's any good,' the blond groans, 'for the first people in space we could have been called something really cool, like, ascension or tsunami or or…'

'Mechtatel,' Nastya smiles, catching me off guard.

It's then the speaker decides to raise its voice again.

'Spaceteam Mechtatel, do you receive? We are ready for launch.'

'Spaceteam Mechtatel receiving, we're ready to go on this end,' Mishka carries on fidgeting with the switches and dials, his face not noticing the sudden name change. But it isn't just him, Marlen has said nothing, neither has Alikhan. Am I going insane? I swear for a moment we were called Vitor's childhood nickname, now it's mine and nobody has batted an eyelid. I know I'm the supposed captain of this Sputnik 1 flight - but I feel like a passenger, not just on this spaceship, but in this entire situation. It's as though everyone in the room knows the punchline to a joke nobody is telling me.

My eyebrows grow angry like Papa's, his fury is about to leave my mouth until the speaker blares again, much louder this time.

'It's time to dance, dance, dance, children, you're on your way!'

The man's words are followed by my body becoming one with the metal chair that I'm sitting in, the force is like nothing I'd ever felt inside Sputnik 0.5. I feel as though I'm going to break down into fine grains of sand and slip through the holes in the chair, before falling out of the cabin to the ground below and getting burnt up in Sputnik 1's scorching hot rocket.

This feeling works completely against the force that pulls us directly upwards into the sky, making my body feel like the colliding of two great powers; an immovable object meets unstoppable force, and with nowhere else for it to go, I pass out.

What feels like Saturday 5th October, 1957.

Somewhere in the LEO (Lower Earth Something), Outer Space.

Sputnik 1 hasn't been fitted with a clock, so I can't tell how long I've been out for, or what day it is, but the groggy feeling inside my head makes it feel as though I've been out for hours. It could be Saturday, or it could still be Friday. I can't tell, time has been passing so strangely since I received the government's letter. I look around the cabin, everyone else has seemingly been out-cold as well and are coming to just as slowly as I am. My eyes wander out of the window, taking in the views of what Papa had called the LEO.

If Sputnik 0.5 was just my imagination, playing in my cardboard spaceship made of make-believe, then I wasn't far off on what space actually looked like. The stars shine so brightly, making the Sun that had snuck in through the windows at Baikonur seem more like a minor inconvenience. I was wrong, they don't look the same as they do from Earth - they're much prettier.

One thing that I didn't count on is the feeling of being so insignificant as I look at the big cloudy ball we get to call home, I can't make out City 40, or Kazan, or Nizhny or Baikonur but for the trail of smoke that looks as though it keeps us tied to the green patches of land below.

'Are we alive?' Marlen asks groggily.

'Of course we're alive,' Mishka laughs, having seemingly been waiting for him to open his mouth and say something stupid.

'We're literally in space and you guys still won't shut up,' Nastya groans.

'Guys, look,' Alikhan points out of the window towards the glimmer that spreads quickly across the top side of the Earth. It starts with a low light, next thing I know the Sun peers out behind, as though it had been hiding from Poschekotat' Ruku.

I can see the faint shadow of a Zilant weaving in and out of the clouds that block our view of the Union, seemingly unaware of us watching it, unaware of how stunning it looked from this angle.

It's the prettiest thing I've ever seen. Well, the second most. I can't help but turn my head away from it, just to look at her again. Nastya catches my gaze and smiles that smile only she can do.

I manage to tear my eyes away and look at Marlen, his lazy eye has already gotten bored of the view and is turning to look at the inside of the cabin.

Mishka pulls a few of the levers on the control panel, causing a machine to poke out of the top of Sputnik 1. My bear focuses the lens of the object on Earth before clicking a small button on the control panel. The camera flash takes us all by surprise, everyone but Mishka that is.

'Job done,' he says, flashing me a furry thumbs up.

'Looks like there was no Moon Force after all,' Nastya says, causing my eyes to glance over to her. She's right, the emptiness of space is deafening, there's no tension like there had been when we were playing pretend in my living room.

I turn back around, soaking it all in. With the whole world in front of me, turning my eyes into miniature globes of blue and green, I look again at my best friends who gaze over it with me. I can't contain my happiness as we watch on from Sputnik 1's cabin. I grab Mishka and pull him into me, squeezing him into my chest like I have done for so many nights in bed at home. Taking it all in for one last time, I close my eyes, never to open them again.

EPILOGUE

On September 29th, 1957, the harrowing Kyshtym Disaster took place. It was an explosion of buried nuclear waste from a plutonium-processing factory named Mayak, near Kyshtym and the secret City 40, where the plant workers lived. The Soviet government refused to acknowledge that this event occurred until 1989 - 32 years later. This is despite 9,000 square miles of land being contaminated, more than 10,000 evacuees being removed from the area and an uncounted number of people who succumbed to the horrific effects of radiation - suspected to be in the hundreds.

Lessons were not learned, and those same mistakes were repeated 29 years later at Chernobyl.

In the years since, Kyshtym has been ranked as a Level 6 disaster on the International Nuclear and

Radiological Event Scale. Only the aforementioned Chernobyl and Fukushima rank higher in their severity.

Just 5 days after the Kyshtym disaster, Sputnik 1, the world's first artificial satellite was launched by the Soviet Union, kickstarting the 'Space Race'.

"Humankind has the science and technology to destroy itself or to provide prosperity for all. But while science offers us these opportunities, science will not make that choice for us."

- Dame Margaret Beckett

If you enjoyed this, why not try Andrew L Cook's other work:

The Toucan Man

'Don't you understand? I'm the Toucan Man – this is my calling. This is what I was put on this Earth to be.'

Ernest Kelly was a simple man. He never yearned for the frivolous aspects of life, just the eternal love of his wife, Eloise. When faced with a tragic loss, Ernest spirals into free-fall, his only direction towards the bottom of the bottle, or a freshly pulled draught pint, pushing away the only family he has left. In his anguish, he stumbles across the superpowers that can give his life meaning again, but only at a cost.

Andrew L. Cook's debut novella tackles themes of grief, addiction and desperation in a world that no longer feels like yours.

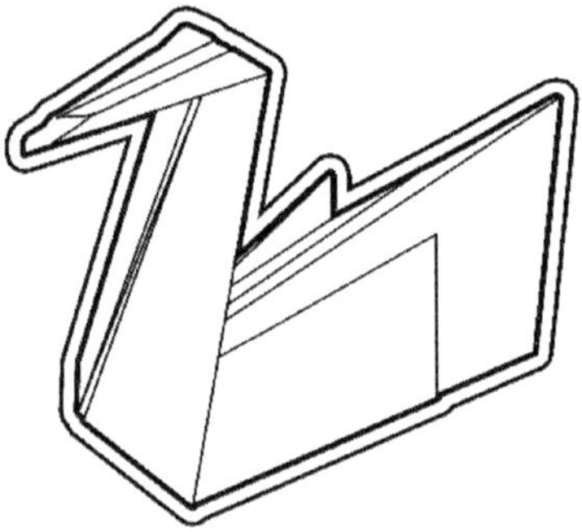

andrewlcookwriter.com

Printed in Great Britain
by Amazon

15554160R00133